industriacide

Volume One

Story & Art by
Sean Dietrich

Letters by
Jay La Valley

Published by

RORSCHACH ENTERTAINMENT

Publisher - James Taylor
Editor - Brian Meredith

Web Address:
www.rorschachentertainment.com

Please Send Comments to:
Info@rorschachentertainment.com

Industriacide Vol. 1 February 2004. Published by Rorschach Entertainment, 3917 170th St. SW, Lynnwood, WA 98037. James Taylor Publisher.

INDUSTRIACIDE FORWARD
By: Matthew Lane

I first saw work on "Industriacide" in 1996, while I was living in Pittsburgh, and yet it was known to have begun some time before that. Seven years is indeed a very long time to be engaged in a single creative endeavor. You may take what you will out of that fact—either Sean Dietrich, Industriacide's creator, has spent his time perfecting his comic debut, or, rather his art has been delayed innumerable times by the torpid realities of life (we've all got bills to pay). To concede that both are true is, I believe, correct. Also correct is the idea that all experience in that interim, from conception to publication, has tempered a stunning work.

I would argue that it has taken these many years for the writer to catch up to the artist. That what knowledge (talent) lacked was wisdom. I have seen Sean in these years through- out the landscapes of Pittsburgh, New Orleans, and now San Diego. A lot of experiences have passed through us, especially in New Orleans where Sean didn't appear to do much work on the comic in the years we spent there. In fact, beyond our steady jobs, the only interests we appeared to pursue were in the bar, hold- ing out empty glasses, beseeching the bartender for another round. This done every time as though we were sure the next double had a for- tune of diamonds at the bottom. Sometimes we found gold. If the toil was going to be our weight in whiskey then the payoff was, or was supposed to be, answers. We met like this, like a committee, holding our culture up to scrutiny and accountability.

You need only look at the work contained herein and you will find it is the product of a man who has been less than satisfied, less than enam- ored with the world around him. Sean's stories are almost supernatu- rally violent. Words and images coalesce into something that if left with an unattended child or an idiot for too long, would undoubtedly prove to have pernicious effects.

INDUSRIACIDE INTRO
by: Richard A. Webster

orgive Sean Dietrich father for he has sinned. Over and over and over again.

once saw him kick a baby rabbit in the ribs. He said its nose wasn't pink enough.

e's a mean little bastard for sure.

it a sin to throw an old lady over the side of a steamboat, because I've seen him do that too.

m not saying he's a bad guy, but he may encounter certain problems come judgement day. To be onest, we all will, including yourself father. It's sin by association and your covered in it.

on't cry father. You'll get used to the feeling. You may even come to enjoy it like Sean Dietrich. He ollects sins like butterflies and drinks tequila like a suicide case.

o, no father, he would never consider suicide. So stop your blubbering. He's too goddamned full of imself. He's got a God-complex. That's probably a sin too, isn't it? Ah well, just put it on his chart. m sure all of this can be sorted out later.

he reason I came to you father is to prepare you and your followers for Industriacide. Fair warning. nce this thing hits the streets you're going to have a packed house and a long line at the confessional. 's going to unearth some buried demons in the minds of your parishioners. Maybe even some in ourself father.

Ve all got them. People like Sean Dietrich and myself, we embrace our demons. They feel like home. Vait, where are you going father? Sit your ass down and let me explain. We're not Satanists, we're ıst deranged and we like the feel of that too.

don't have any nipples. I sold them for $67 to a mother of four. That should earn me some credits ı Heaven, right father? Of course, I suppose I should tell you I blew the $67 on a pygmy whore and 12 pack of Pabst Blue Ribbon. My soul is conflicted.

ı hindsight, maybe I shouldn't have told you that. But you see what I mean when I say that we're eranged.

top that crazy chanting father. I know enough Latin to understand that you're invoking the wrath of ome bloody avenging angel to strike me down. Don't bother. Me and Sean Dietrich made nice with ne of your angels on New Years Eve several years ago in a dirty little bar in New Orleans. She came) deliver us from evil by way of the sword. After seven shots of tequila, she succumbed to our weird harms, pledged to forever protect us from her kin, bid us a fond farewell and went home with a local ervert named Mr. Dingles.

o save your breath father, we've been granted heavenly immunity.

oddammit father, can you stop kissing that crucifix for one second and listen to me.

ean Dietrich is on the eve of releasing his disturbing opus entitled Industriacide and you need to ask ourself this question, what will follow? Once you become comfortable with the answer, you need to repare.

ou look tired father. Don't worry, once I'm done here, after I've been properly intoxicated by the blood f Christ, I will leave you to your internal prayers. But this is important. And don't think I don't ympathize with your task at hand. God's children may be multiplying like rabbits under the cruel eign of Bush Jr., but their minds are weak and highly susceptible to the images and words you will oon discover within the pages of Industriacide. They will be comforted upon the realization that they are not the only ones who feel alone and misunderstood in a dark world that seems bent on their destruction.

I see the scars laced around your wrists, father. I don't pretend to understand your pain, but I am familiar with your motivation. This country, the only home I have ever known, has turned ugly and vicious. It has been overrun by an impotent gang of Jesus-perverts making up for the lack of action in their pants by institutionalizing hatred and blind justice. And the sheep, loyal flock that they are, shuffle along, hating indiscriminately, punishing the fools who refuse to follow.

Proudly, I sit before you father, in this shadowy box constructed to receive and forgive the sins of the sheep, to tell you one thing—I ain't no fucking sheep and neither is Sean Dietrich. I know that scares you but it is something you will have to come to terms with. You got no choice.

Industriacide is just another word to describe the inevitable. But in the heart of Sean Dietrich's creation there exists a long forgotten concept known as free will. It's the only thing worth fighting for. Some may call it repulsive, but not me.

Tormented Schmaltz in an alley, atop a hill of broken femurs and trap-jaw gears, fighting the nightmare, the memory of choking his lush mama with a bottle of gin, blending her brains with an egg-beater. Blood, blood everywhere. There goes the torment.

Beautiful Natalie haunting the dead corridors of the grey Factory pumping pollution into the dumb populace, fueled by the ghostly screams of raped and butchered children. No way out, the whispering assures her, but there has to be, she tells herself. Time for change.

And Jake and that fucking Bear tricking and pushing, heroin spikes inside the belly of that fucking Bear, do it man, Jake you pussy, you shut the fuck up you fucking Bear, but the lights of the rave and that croaking in your veins and stomach, the Hurt, the Hurt, oh yeah, goddamn fucking Bear, I'll show you one day, but not today, maybe when that ambulance runs over me, you fucking Bear, you tricked me and pushed me and the heroin and the lights.....

This is the good stuff. This is truth. Sean Dietrich may not be right in the head but he has a way with spaghetti sauce and coffee grounds.

This world of ours isn't pretty, father. I know your parishioners enjoy waving their flags on the fourth of July, and Monday through Sunday. I know they buy into this neo-con vision of a world free of evil. They believe it can be ushered in through the proper combination of religion, violence and intolerance, but we know better. And it's time you got with the fucking program.

I've listened to your sermons, father. You talk a good game, but to what end?

Industriacide is a wake-up call. Consider me the messenger.

People like Sean Dietrich operate outside of the flock, outside of your reach. That's where the true power lies, and so long as people like him exist, your dumb proclamations amount to so much compost and blended dog shit.

I can see you through the darkened mesh separating my section of the confessional from yours. I can see your bloated eyelids, your trembling lips, your complacency and uncertainty. But can you see where we're coming from?

The next time you flinch, the next time you rub that useless book resting on your genitals, I'm going to launch myself through this fucking curtain and introduce you to the ghosts of our world. It's not something I want to do father, but you're leaving me with little choice.

I knew Sean Dietrich years ago but have since lost track of his poor soul. Word on the street places him in an asylum in Maine where the nuns have been known to wear silk panties, garter belts and fishnet stockings. It's dirty but it's fun.

Oh baby. And that's what we're after. That's Industriacide.

This world is controlled by Bible-thumping zealots who carve scripture into the kidneys of the poor and upon the soft skulls of the newborn while eviscerating the natural world. All in the name of your God. But Sean Dietrich, he got some other ideas, foul thoughts given birth in black and white images reflected in the wide-accepting eyes of the disassociated children howling in his dreams.

Hey father. Guess what? Those little Dietrich kiddies, the windmill weirdos on the loose, unleashed in your community, they're real and they're after your altar boys. But I suppose they will have to get in line, right?

Oh, no. I'm sorry father. That was out of line, wasn't it?

Hey father, rest easy, there's no such thing as a Sean Dietrich or Industriacide. Who would believe such a thing? This mortal world is moving forward, according to the teachings of God and Bush Jr. Everyone is a servant and a sheep.

Forgive me father for I have sinned. I allowed myself to revel in momentary moments in which I worshiped individual freedom, the power of the unbridled spirit, as opposed to knees-on-the-ground subservience. But I'm better now.

Bless me father for I have been original. And that's the worst sin of all.

Yes father, I will say 578 Hail Mary's and 6,421 Our Father's. But first, I will go in search of Sean Dietrich. I will smite him.

Disregard everything you just read. My tongue is raw from licking toads and sucking down cans of Schlitz. My vision is blurred from heavy doses of MDMA and LSD. I tried to stop my fingers from typing this drivel but the coke madness has gotten the better of me.

Nonsense, all of it. Except for the last part.

Sean Dietrich, you scurvy son of a crack addict, I will make you pay for going against the Great Sheep Nation.

Hey, Sean Dietrich, you dirty motherfucker, your godless days are numbered. This here father has assured me that God has forgiven me for our association. My halo has been cleansed of your stink and sharpened to a Biblical razor-like edge.

And that's what we call fair warning.

Fuck Industriacide. And fuck Sean Dietrich.

How about it father?

"Bless you my wayward child."

Goddamn right father. Now let's sell those nipples of yours and get it on with a pygmy whore.

"Amen."

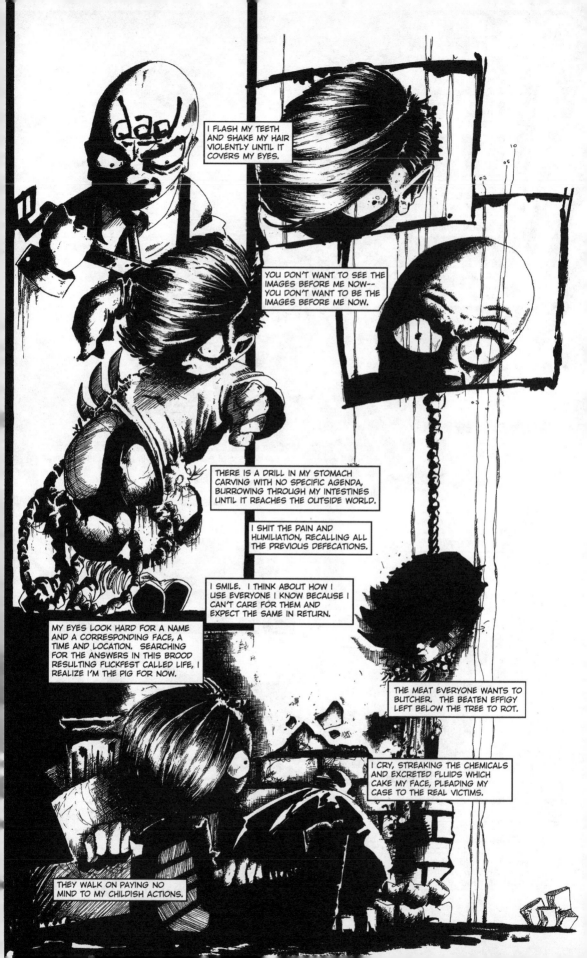

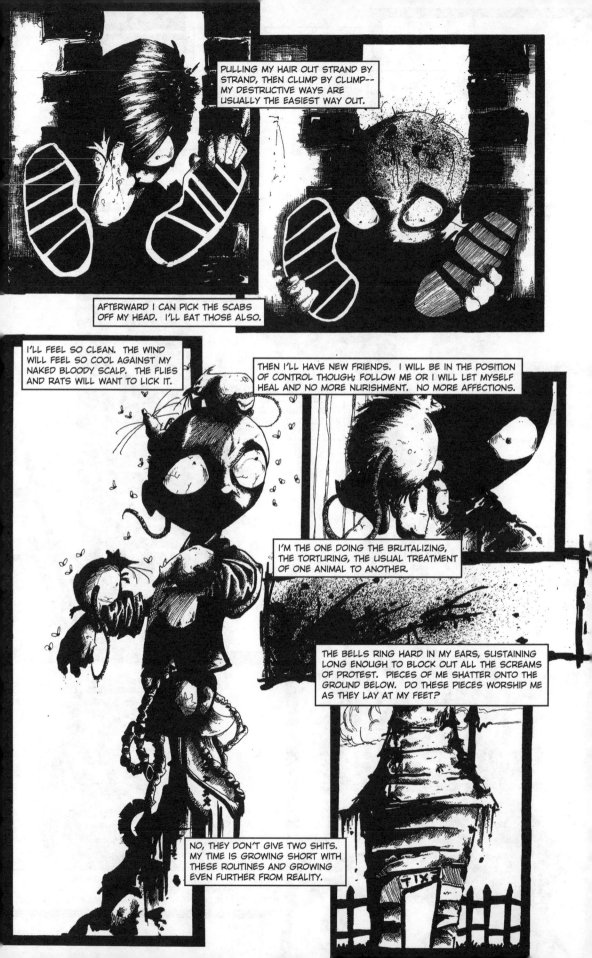

I AM NOTHING BUT A TOY PAINTED BLACK TO MOST ANYWAY.

EVERYTHING I PROCURE IS DONE IN THE MOST PAINFUL MANNER, AND YOU THE DEVIL INSIDE MY HEAD, THE RAT LICKING MY SCALP, THE ROACH SHARING MY LUNCH ARE THE ONLY FRIENDS I HAVE.

MY FEELING THAT YOU DON'T USE ME UNLESS I DESIRE IT RESULTS IN THE OVERLOAD OF THE TEN-THOUSAND OUTLETS OF POWER I'VE BEEN PLUGGED INTO.

SOAKED IN MUD NOW, SITTING IN MY CESSPOOL CUSTOM BUILT FOR THE CONSUMPTION FOR ALL I'VE BECOME, I FEEL THE MUD START TO SLIDE DOWN MY BODY. DOWN MY FACE. DOWN MY NECK. CHEST.

I GET HARD AND PLEASURE MYSELF WITH THOUGHTS OF ALL THOSE WHO THOUGHT I COULD LOVE THEM.

THE SEX WASN'T A SOUL MELDING, IT WAS A WAY OF USING THE MUD FOR LUBRICATION. I SMILE THROUGH THE THICK LAYERS OF GRIME, MY TEETH GLEAMING WHITE.

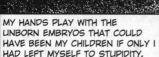

MY HANDS PLAY WITH THE UNBORN EMBRYOS THAT COULD HAVE BEEN MY CHILDREN IF ONLY I HAD LEFT MYSELF TO STUPIDITY.

I RUN MY FINGERS DOWN THE LENGTH OF MY BODY, LETTING THE MUD PACK ITSELF UNDERNEATH MY FINGERNAILS.

TIGHTENING THE TUBES WHICH FEED ME SHIT, I LEARN TO DIRECT THE FLOW STRAIGHT TO MY HEART.

IT DECAYS TOO, MAKING ME FEEL WHOLE AGAIN AS I PART THE MINDS OF OTHERS.

AFTERWARDS I FEEL HOLLOW AND MY STOMACH IS EMPTY. MY SELF INDULGENCE AND EGO FEEDING ALL PLAY A PART IN PURGING ME OF MY CARING FOR EVERY SORROWFUL CASE THAT CROSSES MY PATH.

AS I LAY ON THE GROUND TO GO TO SLEEP, THE BROWN OF MY SKIN AND THE BLOOD WHICH POURS OUT, MAKES MY HANDS SLICK AND I PLEASURE

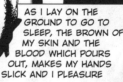

MAYBE IF I THINK THAT I AM PERFECT THEN I WILL BE. EVENTUALLY THE RAIN COVERS ME UP AND WASHES AWAY THE THOUGHT THAT I MIGHT SMOKE A CIGARETTE. SOON SLEEP CATCHES UP WITH ME AND AS I FADE AWAY, I ONLY PRAY THE MUD AND SHIT AND CUM AND BLOOD DON'T SEAL MY EYES SHUT FOR I SO WOULD LIKE TO FUCK MYSELF OVER AGAIN TOMORROW.

OUTSIDE MY DREAM MY ANGER IS STANDING THERE SMILING AT MY EFFORTS BUT INVITING ME TO DIE QUICKLY. I TURN MY BACK TO HER AND CONTINUE TO BATHE IN MY TENETS.

SOON, THOUGH; I TASTE RAINWATER FLOWING INTO ME WITHOUT CONSENT AND I REALIZE I CAN'T MOVE. IT STARTS WITH A SECTION OF SKIN, BUT SPREADS TO ALL PARTS OF MY BODY.

MY RATS AND FLIES AND ROACHES ARE NO LONGER AROUND. MY FAITH HAS COLLAPSED. MY IDEAS AND PLANS HAVE BEEN STOLEN BY THE CLOCK.

I BECOME THE ALLEYS FOOD, ANOTHER MEAL FOR WHEN MY FRIENDS CONTINUE ON. ANOTHER MEMORY LOST. THE SUNSET ABOVE ME IS BLUE AND THEN BLACK.

ANOTHER LOST VISION. FOR NOW THOUGH IT'S TIME TO WRAP MYSELF IN NEWSPAPER AND SAY FAREWELL. AS I FLOAT DOWN THE RIVER IN THE ALLEY, I CAN SEE YOU ON THE RIVER BANKS OF MANY YEARS AGO.

YOU ARE STANDING WITH YOUR SLAVEBOY AND A BOTTLE OF WHISKEY, THE BOTH OF YOU LAUGHING. CRUSTY THINGS START TO FORM IN THE CORNERS OF MY EYES.

WHEN THE FIRST FEW RAINDROPS HIT STARTED TO FALL, AN ARMY OF UMBRELLAS EXTENDED TO FULL SPAN WITH SMALL BAYONETTES ON THE TOPS, PROTECTING THE PEOPLE AND THEIR PARCELS FROM THE ONSLAUGHT OF THE RAIN.

UNDER OVERHANGS, INTO STORES IN WHICH THEY HAVE NO BUSINESS, OR INTO COFFEEHOUSES FOR A DRINK THEY SUDDENLY HAVE THE URGE FOR.

LIKE RATS OVER PILES OF GARBAGE THEY RUN. I'M INTRIGUED FOR THE MOMENT, BUT THAT SOON PASSES.

I CONCENTRATE ON ME. THERE IS MY RELAXATION. MY WORMS. I DON'T REQUIRE HIDING UNDER THE VASTNESS OF AN UMBRELLA, OR THE MENU OF A COFFEEHOUSE.

I AM CONTENT WITH MY THOUGHTS AND THE DIZZYING SMELL OF OIL AND WASTE. I REST FROM MY NIGHTMARES OF THE PREVIOUS NIGHT.

I REST FROM MY ESCAPE FROM A HOSPITAL. WATCHING THE STEAM RISE FROM MY STYROFOAM SMOKESTACK CUP, I SLIP INTO THE LAST TIME I DO REMEMBER RAIN.

I RECALL JUST HOW I ENDED UP WITH AN OPPORTUNITY TO BE PUT INTO A HOSPITAL FROM WHICH I COULD ESCAPE.

A CHARCOAL MESS OF STEEL AND
BRICK CONTRASTING THE SKY,
EMITTING A CACOPHONY OF
COUNTLESS PROCESSES ONGOING
FROM WITHIN THE STRUCTURE.

SMOKE, THE USUAL WASTE
MATERIAL, BLOATS THE ONCE
BLUE SKY TO A SICKENING
GRAY. OTHER THAN THAT IT
IS STILL. NOTHING AT ALL.

EVERY ONCE IN A WHILE A TRUCK WILL
DRIVE AWAY WITH A LOAD OF ELECTRONIC
DEVICES TO SELL TO THE "CONVINCED BY
ADVERTISING" CONSUMERS.

THOSE PEOPLE, THOUGH; ARE JUST
AS FEARFUL OF THE FACTORY WHICH
SPREADS ITS MECHANICAL SHADOW,
THE MARCH OF INDUSTRIAL
PROGRESS, ACROSS THE TOWN.

IT IS EVIDENT BY THE DIRT SMEARS
AND AGED IRON THAT THIS
FACTORY HAS OUTLIVED MANY
PURPOSES AND THE INTENTION TO
STOP SOON IS NOT AN OPTION.

IT ALMOST AT ITS OWN WILL
TURNS THE GEARS OF THE
MACHINES, SLAVE TO NO ONE'S
MANUFACTURING SCHEDULE.

IT IS CHANGING THOUGH. NOT
PHYSICALLY BUT MENTALLY. AND
NOT ITSELF. IT'S CHANGING A
TEN YEAR OLD BOY.

HIS NAME IS SCHMALTZ. HIS CLOTHES MATCH THE FACTORY'S GRAYNESS AND THE BLACK STREAKS OF AGE AS HE WATCHES FROM THE OPPOSING HILL.

THE ENTHRALLMENT OF THE FACTORY'S PHYSIQUE AND THE DISCHARGE OF SMOKE STARTED WHEN HE WAS YOUNGER.

IT HAS GROWN TO ALTER HIS MENTAL STATE.

MESSAGES HEARD FORM WITHIN THE BRICK SHELL ITSELF, THE MACHINES TRYING TO CONVERSE WITH HIM ON A LEVEL TRANSMITTED THROUGH POLLUTANTS, AND THROUGH THE

SHAPES IN THE CLOUDS OF SMOKE, THICK WITH CRAP, POINT HIM IN DIRECTIONS OF WHICH HE WOULD NEVER CONCIEVE OF ON HIS OWN.

VIOLENT ACTS TO BE PERFORMED AS SOON AS POSSIBLE TO PERHAPS FURTHER A MOVEMENT OF SOME SORT. BITS OF MURDER AND LUST DRIVEN BLOODSHED APPEAR BEFORE HIS EYES.

HIS IMAGINATION TOOK OVER AND FORMULATED THE REST OF THE PLANS TO CARRY OUT THE SUGGESTED PLAN IN LIFE.

IT WAS CHANGING HIM YES, BUT NONE OF THE TWO PARTIES KNEW IT YET.

THE FACTORY, 'CIDE INC., PROGRAMMED TO DO IT'S DUTIES AS IT HAS FOR THE LAST 80 YEARS, AND SCHMALTZ UNKNOWINGLY ALTERED BY ILLUSIONS THOUGHT TO BE REAL.

THERE WAS A THIRD PARTY CONTRIBUTING TO SCHMALTZ'S METAMORPHOSIS...HIS MOTHER.

DAY TO DAY LIFE WAS ROUTINE BUT SLIGHTLY ASKEW.

SCHMALTZ'S MOM PAID HER BILLS, GROCERY SHOPPED WITH COUPONS, AND HAD A SET NUMBER OF TELEVISION PROGRAMS TO ENTERTAIN HER. THE REST OF THE TIME WAS SPENT ON HER LITTLE BOY.

WITH DAD LONG OUT OF THE PICTURE, SHE WAS FREE TO MOLD A CHILD FREE OF ALL OUTSIDE INFLUENCES. MOST OF THE MOLDING AND FORMING WAS CAME AFTER A COUPLE OF BOTTLES OF GIN AFTER DINNER.

MOMMY HAD NO ROOM IN HER AGENDA FOR SCHMALTZ'S FACTORY EITHER.

EVERYTIME SHE FOUND OUT THAT HE HAD BEEN SPENDING TIME ON HIS HILL WATCHING THE FACTORY, SHE BEAT HIM.

AND THE BLOOD DID FLOW. THIS FASCINATION WITH 'CIDE INC. CAME TO HER ATTENTION THROUGH A JOURNAL ENTRY SHE FOUND IN HIS ROOM.

THE DRAWINGS, WRITINGS, AND OTHER NOTATIONS TOLD OF A BOY TORTURED BY HIS MOTHER, AND TURNING TO THE FACTORY FOR COMFORT.

SHE REACTED IN HER NORMAL WAY, BUT THIS TIME HE RAN OFF, OUT INTO THE RAIN, AND NOT TO BE SEEN FOR ANOTHER DAY.

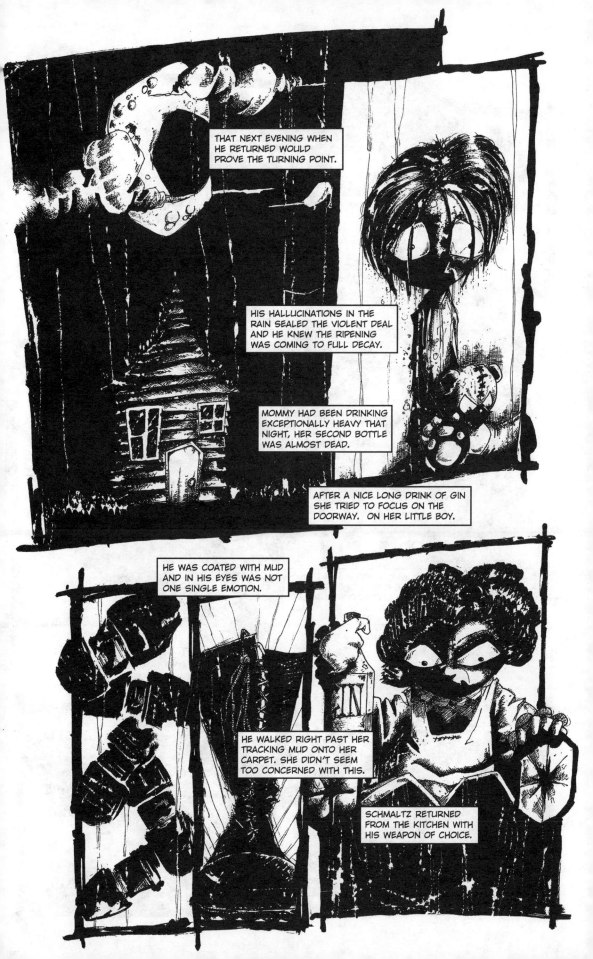

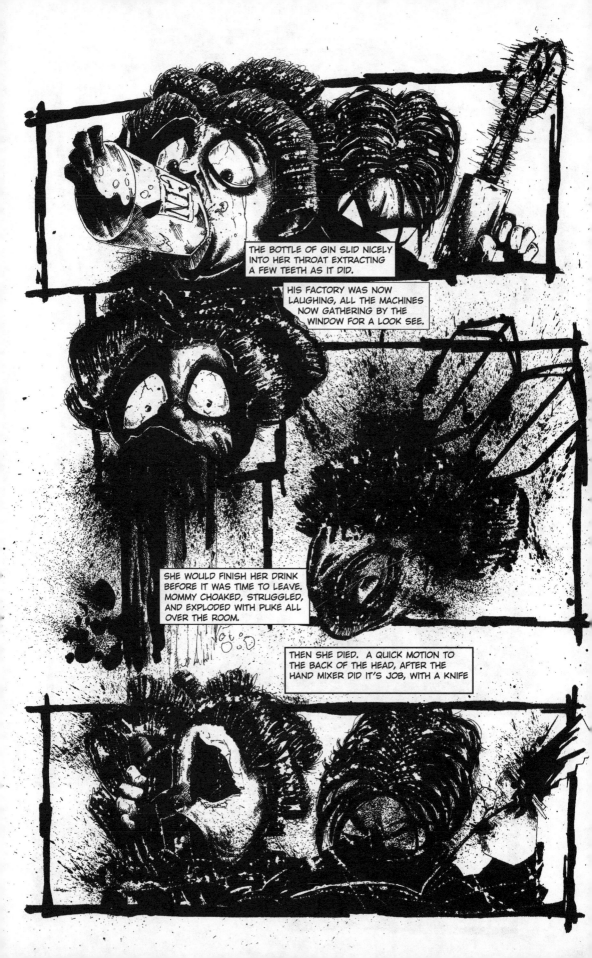

WHEN THE POLICE FOUND HIM THE NEXT DAY HE WAS HAVING COFFEE ON THE STOOP OF AN ABANDONED HOUSE. HIS TEDDY BEAR WAS THERE, AND SO WAS THE HEAD OF MOMMY.

SCHMALTZ WAS COATED WITH BLOOD AND SOME OF THE MUD FROM LAST NIGHT'S RAIN.

HIS THOUGHTS WERE OFF IN SOME DISTANT ORBIT AROUND A FAR AWAY EMOTION.

THEY PUT HIM IN A VAN AND TOOK HIM TO A MENTAL HOSPITAL ON THE EDGE OF TOWN.

HE SOON FOUND OUT THAT THIS PLACE HAD NOTHING TO DO WITH HEALING.

NATALIE HAS THE ABILITY TO GO MAD OVER THIS FACTORY. OVER THE MACHINES. THE THOUGHT OF HER DAD'S DEATH LEADING TO THE INHERITANCE OF THIS HAUNTED MEMORY DROWNS HER IN THE SWEAT AND BLOOD PUT INTO THIS PLACE.

IT'S A TIRING ROUTINE, THIS BANE SHE DEALS WITH EVERY NIGHT, TRYING TO APPEASE WHOEVER IS INSIDE HER HEAD, BUT A ROUTINE WHICH OFFERS FRESH ANNOYANCE EVERY NIGHT.

AS SLEEP TAKES OVER HER TENETS, SHE SLEEPWALKS IN HER DREAMS, FOLLOWING THEM THROUGH THEIR INEXTRICABLE LEAD.

DOWN STAIRS THAT DON'T EXIST, SHE SEES PREVIOUS LIVES AND ENCOUNTERS THROUGH THE EYES OF THE MACHINES.

80 YEARS AGO THE MAIN PART OF THE BUILDING USED TO BE

COWS, CHICKENS, MOSTLY PIGS, TAKEN THROUGH THE MAIN DOORS AND GUTTED FOR THEIR SWEET PRIZE.

THE SCREAMS OF THE PIGS DROWN OUT HER SLIGHT NOISE OF SHOCK SHE PRODUCES WHEN THE IMAGES OF THE PIGS MANIFEST.

EACH AND EVERY SOUL AND SOULESS TORMENTOR EXTRACT THEIR HURT ON NATALIE'S EARS, AND SHE DIZZIES FROM THE SMELL.

IT STARTS TO DIE OUT EVENTUALLY, BUT NOT BEFORE LEAVING HER IN A FRANTIC STATE OF DISBELIEF.

WHERE THESE APPARITIONS CAME FROM ALL AT ONCE IS MINDBOGGLING. WHO WOULD DO SUCH THINGS TO CHILDREN?

WHO WOULD POINT AND SAY YOU ARE TO BEAR THE WEIGHT OF RAPE AND TORTURE? WHO WOULD CONSUME SO MUCH SWINE?

THE THOUGHT OF PEOPLE SITTING AT THEIR DINNER TABLES ACROSS AMERICA, THEIR FACES STUFFED IN A NEVERENDING SEA OF SWINE IS TOO MUCH.

KIDS EATING IT OUT OF DOG BOWLS AND SIX INCHES OF BLOOD AND FAT AT THEIR FEET SLOWLY SWIRLING IN THE AIR CURRENTS FINALLY DOES IT FOR HER.

NAUSEA TAKES OVER AND SHE SNAPS OUT OF HER OWN INTERNAL DISCOURSE FINDING HERSELF CRYING. SHE IS ALONE. SHE IS UNNERVED AND TWITCHING. NATALIE KNOWS IT'S TIME FOR A CHANGE.

NICHOLS 1200 SUPERS. TOP OF THE LINE TURNTABLES. STACKS OF VINYL. A RAVE OF SORTS. A BILLION COLORS FLASH IN THE RETINAS OF HUNDREDS OF KID'S EYES.

OTHER COLORS FLASH, TRAILING ACROSS THE VISUAL PATH, DRUG INDUCED WARPING OF THE ROOM.

NICHOLS 1200 SUPERS

MONSTROUS SOUND ADDING BEATS TO THE HEARTS OWN, PUSHING AUDITORY SENSORY INPUT TO PEAK LEVELS.

THE DANCE. TALK. TRIP. THEY BASK IN THEIR OWN SELF-FOUND SPIRITUALITY OF IT ALL INSIDE OF THIS TEMPLE CLUB OF NON-DENOMINATION.

THE HEAT IS ON A STEADY RISE AS MORE PEOPLE ARRIVE. DISCUSSIONS ONCE PICKED UP ON FROM JUST A FEW FEET AWAY, NOW ONLY MOUTHS MOVING WITHOUT WORDS.

PLUSH VELVET CHAIRS FOR THE TIRED. STOCKED BAR FOR THE THIRSTY.

ALL AROUND AN AIR OF LOST BLISS NEWLY FOUND BY THOSE WHO PERHAPS HAVE JUST ENDED THEIR WORK WEEK, OR THOSE WHO JUST HAVE REALLY GOOD DRUGS. EITHER OF THE RESULTS ARE OF A COMMON FEELING.

MOBY

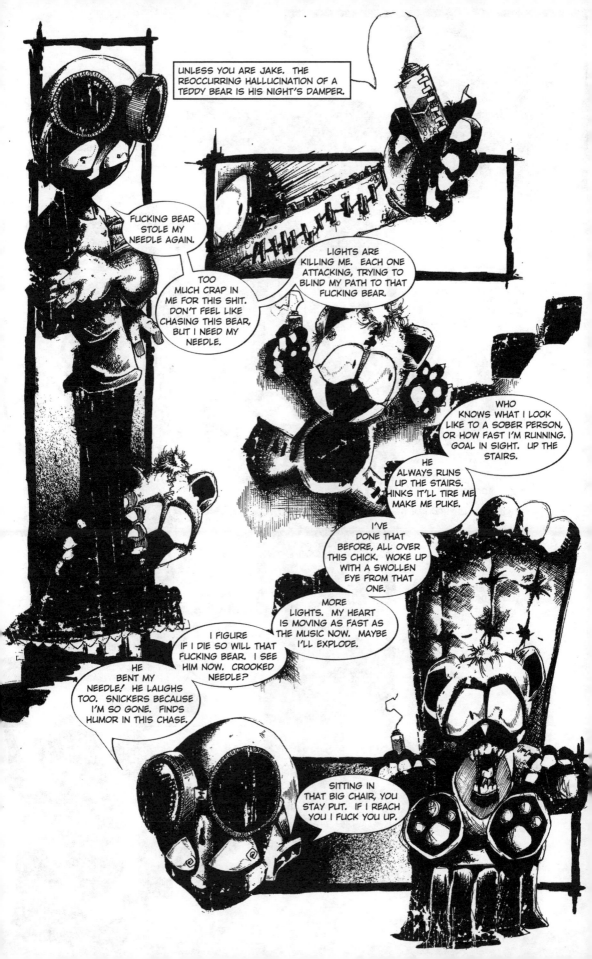

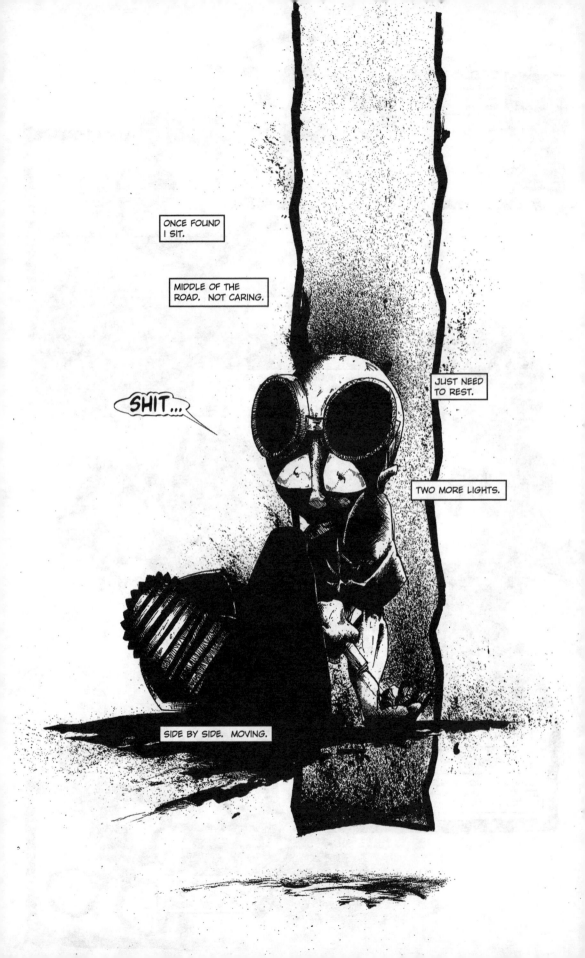

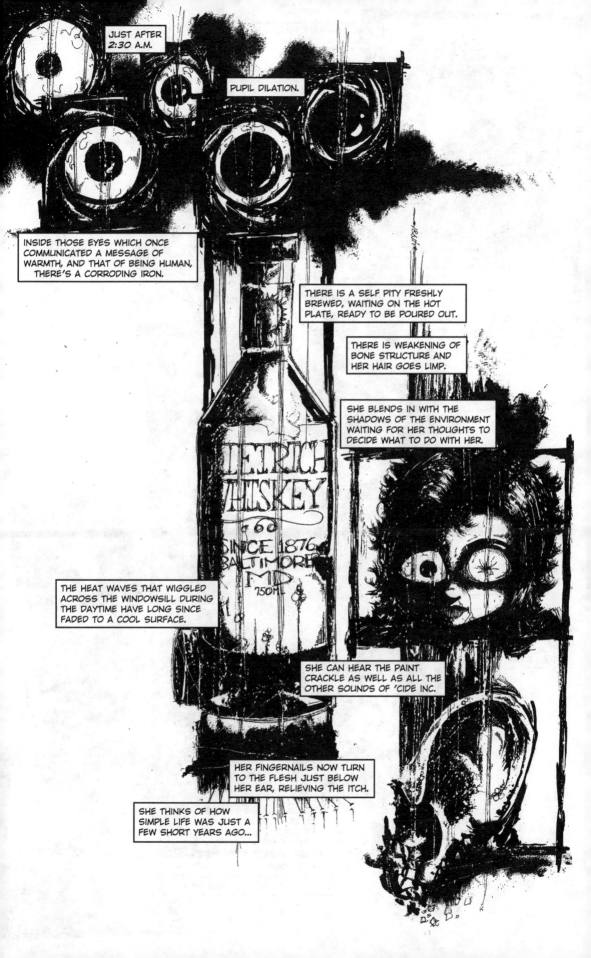

JUST AFTER 2:30 A.M.

PUPIL DILATION.

INSIDE THOSE EYES WHICH ONCE COMMUNICATED A MESSAGE OF WARMTH, AND THAT OF BEING HUMAN, THERE'S A CORRODING IRON.

THERE IS A SELF PITY FRESHLY BREWED, WAITING ON THE HOT PLATE, READY TO BE POURED OUT.

THERE IS WEAKENING OF BONE STRUCTURE AND HER HAIR GOES LIMP.

SHE BLENDS IN WITH THE SHADOWS OF THE ENVIRONMENT WAITING FOR HER THOUGHTS TO DECIDE WHAT TO DO WITH HER.

THE HEAT WAVES THAT WIGGLED ACROSS THE WINDOWSILL DURING THE DAYTIME HAVE LONG SINCE FADED TO A COOL SURFACE.

SHE CAN HEAR THE PAINT CRACKLE AS WELL AS ALL THE OTHER SOUNDS OF 'CIDE INC.

HER FINGERNAILS NOW TURN TO THE FLESH JUST BELOW HER EAR, RELIEVING THE ITCH.

SHE THINKS OF HOW SIMPLE LIFE WAS JUST A FEW SHORT YEARS AGO...

DIETRICH WHISKEY
SINCE 1876
BALTIMORE MD
750ML

MUCH OF HER PAST FLOODS BACK IN A CACOPHONY OF WHY'S AND I CAN'T. NO FUTURE IN PITY AND WORTHLESSNESS, SHE TRIES TO PLAN THE NEXT MOVE.

IT DOESN'T COME.

SHE THEN SEES A DOLL OFF IN THE CORNER. BURNT IN SOME PLACES, SHE DOESN'T REMEMBER IT EVER BEING THERE, BUT LIKE MOST THINGS IN 'CIDE INC. SHE EXPECTS THEM TO APPEAR WITHOUT WARNING.

THE DOLL SPEAKS IN THE SAME TONE, NO EXPRESSION, NOT CHANGING, BUT CAUSING SOMETHING IN THE GIRL. MAYBE A SPARK OF HOPE OR SOME WARMTH RETURNING TO THOSE IRON CORRODING EYES.

THE DOLL SPEAKING AS THE FACTORY'S PERSONA, OPENING A WINDOW TO CIRCULATE THE STALE AIR.

A FRESH BLOOD PUMPS.

THE GROAN OF THE MACHINE ECHOES THROUGH HER HALLWAYS OF SELF WORTH AND SHE SMILES.

A SHOT OF OIL ON THE GEARS, WHISKEY FOR THE THROAT. SLOWLY TURNING FORWARD. THE CLEARING OF COBWEBS. THE SOLO IN THE CHOIR. NOTE BY NOTE ORCHESTRATING HER FINAL MECHANIZED SYMPHONIC WAR.

OUTSIDE HER WINDOW THE PEOPLE OF THE CITY, ANT-LIKE IN APPEARANCE, MOVE UNAWARE OF THEIR SELF-PERPETRATING ABDICATION.

NO REMORSE FOR THE MONKEYS THEY'VE BECOME, ENDLESS CASH FLOW, HOLLOW SPENDING. CARBON COPIES OF CELEBRITY FASHIONS AND COMMERCIAL BREAKS, THEIR PIG NOSES HIDDEN UNDER SKIN CARE PRODUCTS.

EVERYDAY 'CIDE INC. PRODUCES ELECTRONICS FOR THEM. LOUDER SPEAKERS. FASTER COMPUTERS. FUTURISTIC DESIGN DOING ANCIENT TASKS.

A LONG TIME AGO NATALIE'S FUSE BLEW IN HER HEAD WHICH COULD SOMEHOW JUSTIFY BEING PART OF THIS.

THE DREAMS SHE HAS TORTURE HER AT NIGHT AND MANIFEST IN HUMAN FOR DURING NORMAL BUSINESS HOURS.

EACH CHECK THAT IS WRITTEN, EACH CREDIT CARD THAT IS VERIFIED, EACH WAD OF CASH RUSTLED OUT OF A POCKET, MARCHES SADISTICALLY IN LINE FOLLOWED BY THE WHISKEY BOTTLE WHICH SOOTHES THE GUILT.

THE SHOT GLASS HITS THE TABLE AND FALLS TO THE FLOOR. PEN. PAPER.

NATALIE FOLLOWS TO THE HARDWOOD BELOW AND BEGINS HER BIRTHING PROCESS. IDEAS. TIMES. TONNAGE OF METAL NECESSARY FOR THE PROJECT.

SHE IS NOW CONTROLLED BY INTERNAL FORCES--CONTROLLED BY THE HATRED FOR WHAT DADDY LEFT FOR HER TO DEAL WITH.

THE FIERCENESS OF HER MOTIONS ON THE PAPER DRIVEN BY THE WHISKEY SLOWLY FORMS THE MARROW OF HER PLAN.

THE PIGS ARE GETTING EXITED NOW.

DADDY SHIFTS IN HIS GRAVE.

THE FACTORY'S WORKERS ARE SWEATY AND FILLED WITH ANGER.

THEY ARE READY TO PUT IN A HARD DAYS WORK.

THEY ARE READY TO RELIEVE THE AGGRESSION.

TWO HOURS LATER
SHE IS DONE.

EVERYWHERE SHE LOOKS
TELEVISIONS ARE EXPLODING,
TOYS ARE EATING EACH OTHER,
AND CREDIT CARDS ARE
MELTING FROM HER ENERGY.

DADDY FALLS BACK ASLEEP IN
HIS GRAVE WITH DEPRESSION
AS THE SEDATIVE.

EVERYWHERE NATALIE LOOKS
PEOPLE ARE GETTING WHAT
THEY DESERVE.

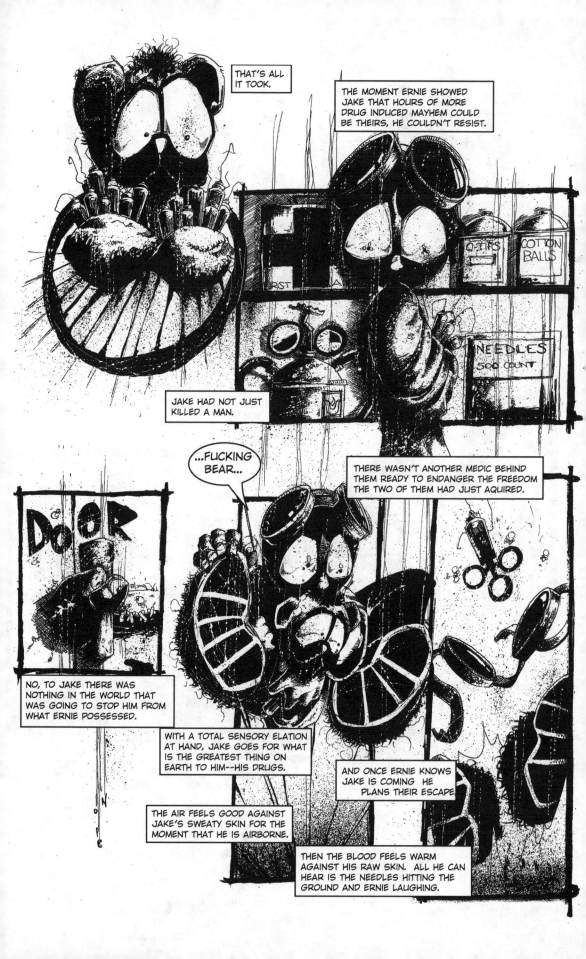

THE STAINED COLORS ON THE CANVAS NOW TURN BLACK AND WHITE, A STORMY CLIMAX IN THIS FILM.

HER BEAUTY SHATTERS INSIDE AND NATURAL FUCKING NOISE.

THE ELEMENTS WHICH DESTROY MY PLAYTHINGS MOVE TO A SHEET METAL BEAT, MIMICKING THE KNIVES PUSHED INTO ME.

I PULL EACH ONE OUT LICKING THEM SLOWLY SMILING AT YOU.

TELLING YOU I CAN TAKE EVERY MALIGNANT TUMOR YOU PUT IN MY BRAIN.

IN THE END THOUGH WHEN YOU FINALLY END ALL COMMUNICATION, AND CUT THE NETWORK BETWEEN US, I REALIZE THE HOLE I'M IN.

THE VAST EXPANSE ACROSS MY FRONTAL LOBE FILLS WITH THE GOOD MEMORIES, SYSTEMATICALLY ELIMINATING THE DETRIMENTAL TIME WE HAD.

theres no way of reviving this without somehow turning blue to pale stale to everyone I rape. My fears reside in you with my looks...

EVENTUALLY ALL I HAVE LEFT ARE THE WORDS I WROTE AFTER THE UMBILICAL CORD WAS CUT, MY HEART IN A FREE FALL, INCREASING IN SPEED AS IT TURNS TO A HARDER ROCK...

MY VOMIT OFFERS THE RECOURSE
MY NERVES WERE LOOKING FOR.

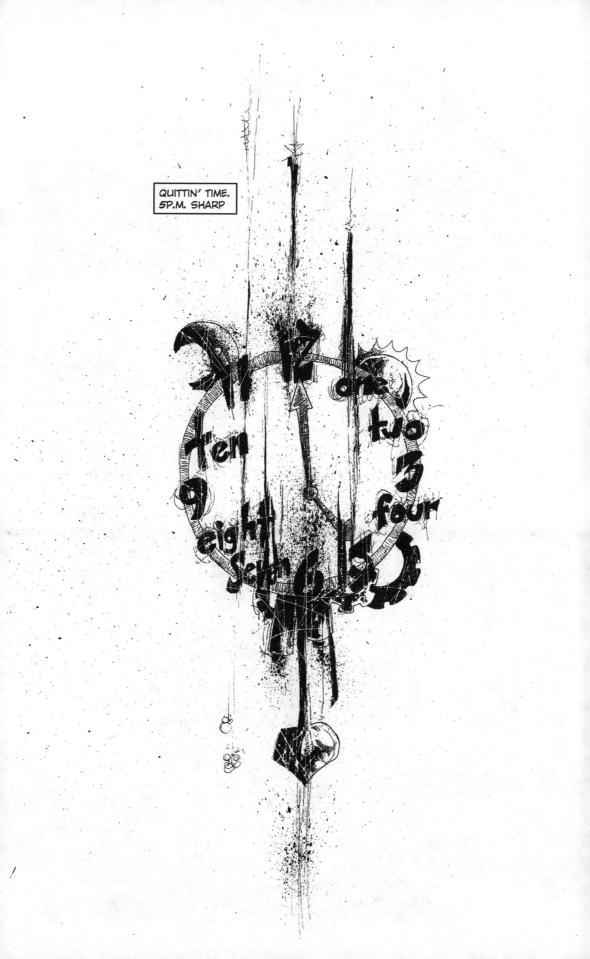

QUITTIN' TIME.
5P.M. SHARP

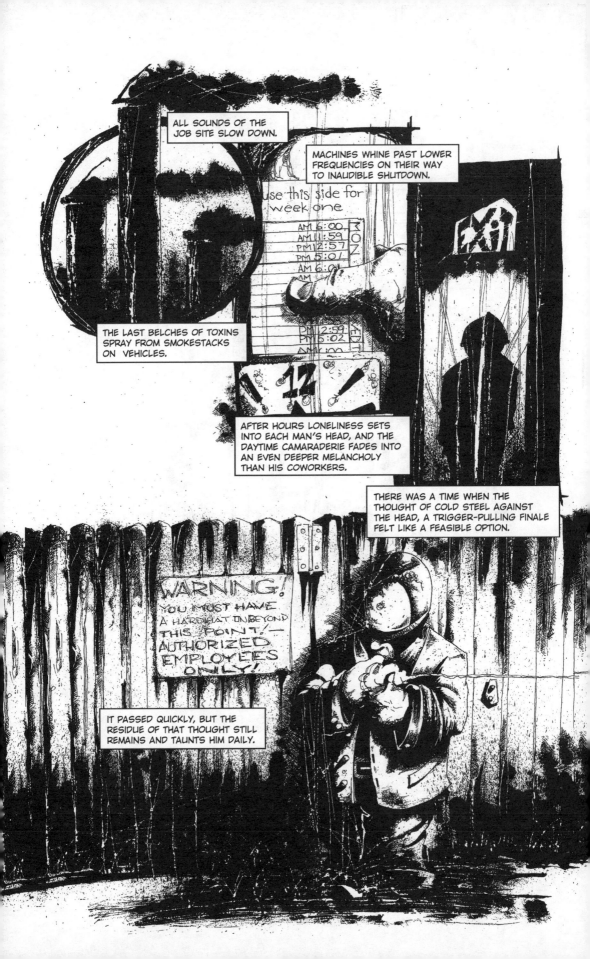

ALL SOUNDS OF THE JOB SITE SLOW DOWN.

MACHINES WHINE PAST LOWER FREQUENCIES ON THEIR WAY TO INAUDIBLE SHUTDOWN.

THE LAST BELCHES OF TOXINS SPRAY FROM SMOKESTACKS ON VEHICLES.

AFTER HOURS LONELINESS SETS INTO EACH MAN'S HEAD, AND THE DAYTIME CAMARADERIE FADES INTO AN EVEN DEEPER MELANCHOLY THAN HIS COWORKERS.

THERE WAS A TIME WHEN THE THOUGHT OF COLD STEEL AGAINST THE HEAD, A TRIGGER-PULLING FINALE FELT LIKE A FEASIBLE OPTION.

IT PASSED QUICKLY, BUT THE RESIDUE OF THAT THOUGHT STILL REMAINS AND TAUNTS HIM DAILY.

ONCE HE REACHES THE FRONT DOOR, ONE MORE GLANCE AT THE STREWN PLAYHOUSE CAUSES THE REALIZATION THAT THIS PLAY DOES NOT END, BUT WILL BOTHER HIM CONTINUALLY.

THE WHIRRING OF THE CAN OPENER, ANOTHER MECHANISM ORCHESTRATING HIS LIFE, BACKING VOCALS TO HIS QUESTIONS, BREAKS THE SILENCE.

A WET SLAP OF SOUP INTO THE PAN, LIKE THE BUM HITTING THE WET CARDBOARD OF HOME, AND DINNER IS ON.

CLIMAX OF MEMORIES HITS ED, JUST ABOUT DINNERTIME, WHEN HE REMEMBERS HER MEALS.

EVERYDAY A WARM MEAL AND A HUG FROM HIS SON.

ARGUMENT OVER PEAS?

"YOU'LL GROW UP BIG AND STRONG LIKE ME," USUALLY ENDED THAT.

IT'S THE PICTURE ABOVE THE MANTEL, THOUGH, WHICH BOLTS THAT FEELING OF LOSS TO THE HEART WITH EVER INCREASING PERMANENCE.

THUMBING IT WITH AFFECTION EVERY NIGHT, CRYING OUT TO WHATEVER CAUSTIC GROWTH IS WITHIN HIM, HE CAN'T REMEMBER THE LAST TIME HE WASN'T FULLY CLOTHED WHEN HE WOKE IN THE MORNING.

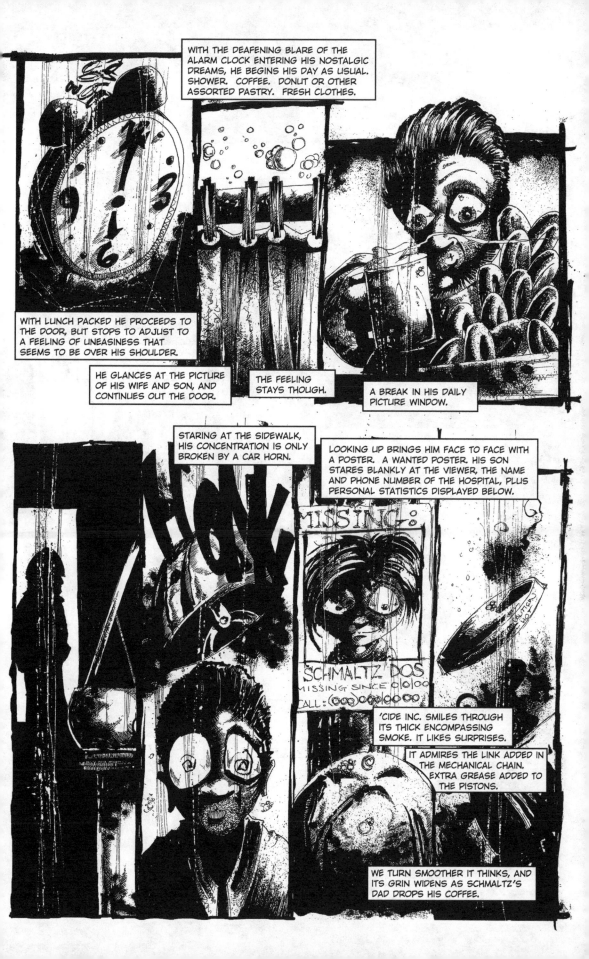

WITH THE DEAFENING BLARE OF THE ALARM CLOCK ENTERING HIS NOSTALGIC DREAMS, HE BEGINS HIS DAY AS USUAL. SHOWER. COFFEE. DONUT OR OTHER ASSORTED PASTRY. FRESH CLOTHES.

WITH LUNCH PACKED HE PROCEEDS TO THE DOOR, BUT STOPS TO ADJUST TO A FEELING OF UNEASINESS THAT SEEMS TO BE OVER HIS SHOULDER.

HE GLANCES AT THE PICTURE OF HIS WIFE AND SON, AND CONTINUES OUT THE DOOR.

THE FEELING STAYS THOUGH.

A BREAK IN HIS DAILY PICTURE WINDOW.

STARING AT THE SIDEWALK, HIS CONCENTRATION IS ONLY BROKEN BY A CAR HORN.

LOOKING UP BRINGS HIM FACE TO FACE WITH A POSTER. A WANTED POSTER. HIS SON STARES BLANKLY AT THE VIEWER, THE NAME AND PHONE NUMBER OF THE HOSPITAL, PLUS PERSONAL STATISTICS DISPLAYED BELOW.

MISSING:

SCHMALTZ DOS
MISSING SINCE 0|0|00
CALL: (000) 000|00 00

'CIDE INC. SMILES THROUGH ITS THICK ENCOMPASSING SMOKE. IT LIKES SURPRISES.

IT ADMIRES THE LINK ADDED IN THE MECHANICAL CHAIN. EXTRA GREASE ADDED TO THE PISTONS.

WE TURN SMOOTHER IT THINKS, AND ITS GRIN WIDENS AS SCHMALTZ'S DAD DROPS HIS COFFEE.

NOW, STANDING ON TOP OF THIS FIRE ESCAPE, SCHMALTZ IS VISITED BY THAT SAME FEELING HE HAD WHEN HE CLIMBED OUT OF THE DRAINAGE DITCH NOT TOO LONG AGO AND LOOKED WESTWARD.

HIS BUDDY STARES AT HIM WITH A WELCOMING SMILE.

HIS FRIEND. THE REASON HE KILLED HIS MOMMY. THE REASON HE WENT TO THE HOSPITAL IN THE FIRST PLACE. 'CIDE INC.

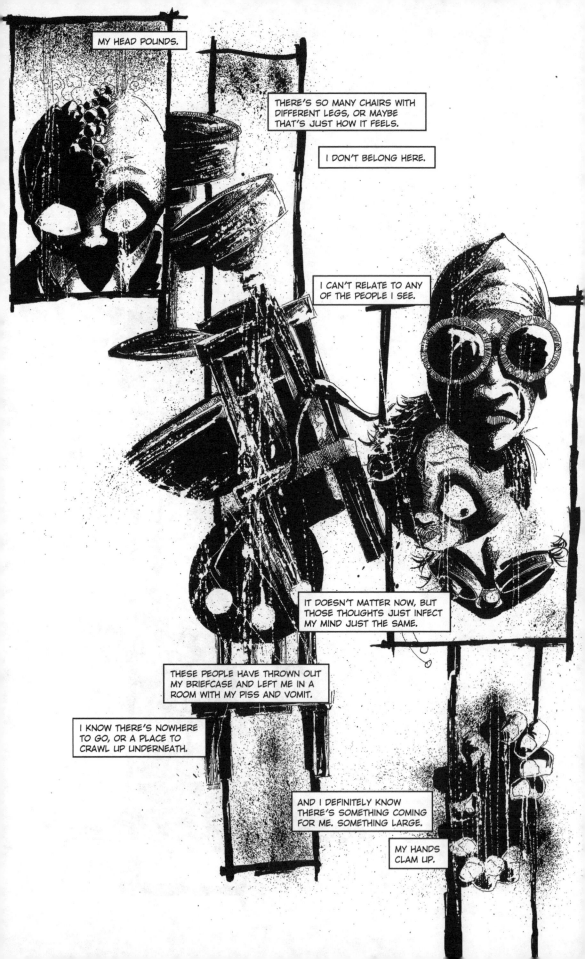

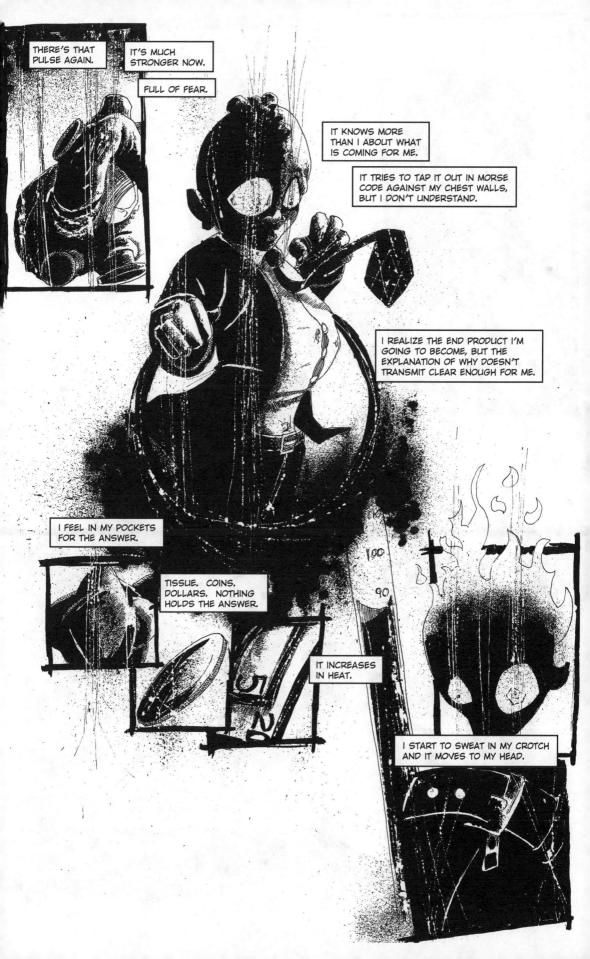

ONCE UPON A TIME IN THE UPPER LEVEL OF AN OLD ABANDONED APARTMENT BUILDING, THERE LIVED A LITTLE GIRL.

AND ONCE UPON THAT SAME TIME THERE WAS HER NEEDLE PRINCE.

HE HAD COME DOWN WITH A TERRIBLE SICKNESS THOUGH, AND EVERYDAY SHE MADE IT HER NUMBER ONE PRIORITY TO TAKE CARE OF HIM IN HOPES THAT ONE DAY HE WOULD AWAKEN AND THEY WOULD PLAY TOGETHER.

SHE KEPT HIS GOGGLES CLEAN AND SAFE.

SHE FED HIM SOUP EVEN THOUGH HE WOULD FALL ASLEEP HALFWAY THROUGH DINNER.

SHE SAT IN THE CORNER OF THE ROOM AND CRIED FOR THE DAY HE WOULD FINALLY WAKE UP.

MOST OF ALL THOUGH, SHE LIKED TO READ TO HIM.

SHE FELT THAT IF SHE READ TALES OF MAGIC AND ADVENTURE TO HIM OUT LOUD, THEN HE WOULD DREAM THE MOST WONDERFUL DREAMS.

AND MAYBE. JUST MAYBE. THOSE WONDERFUL DREAMS WOULD END AND JAKE WOULD FINALLY BE READY TO AWAKEN.

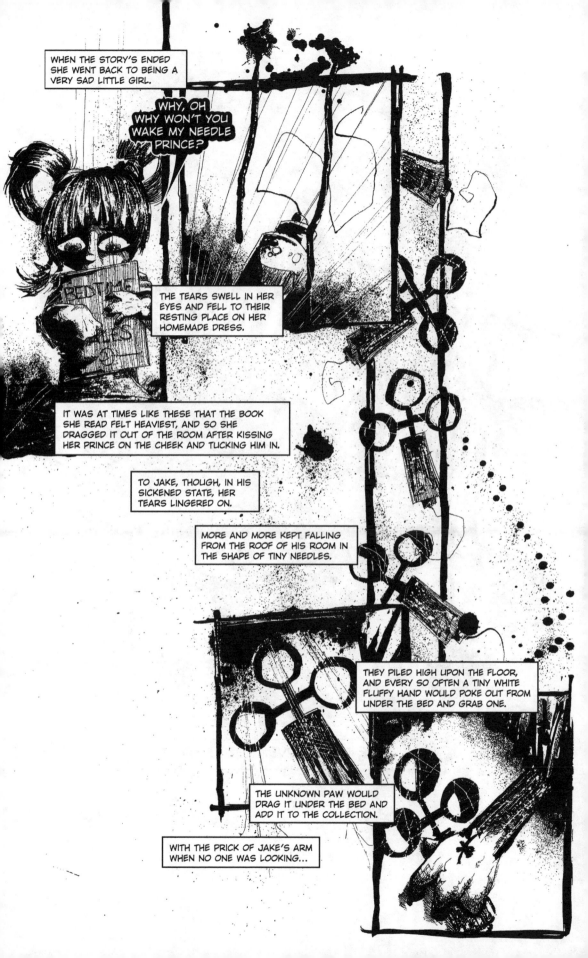

...THE REAL ADVENTURE BEGINS.

CLICK

THE PUSH OF THE BUTTON BY A LATEX HAND SENDS THE ELECTRICAL CURRENT ALONG THE RIGHT PATH.

THE PATH WHICH WILL START THE PROCESS OF TURNING A NORMAL NIGHT INTO SOMETHING MORE.

THE PREPARATIONS FOR THE EVENTS TO FOLLOW WERE NOT WELL THOUGHT OUT, MERELY THROWN TOGETHER BY THE DETERMINED MIND OF A PERSON WHO HAS GIVEN UP ON ALL HER EYES CAN SEE.

FOR THE NIGHTTIME JANITOR, IT'S ALREADY BEEN AN INTERESTING EVENING.

HIS PAYCHECK WILL STATE, AS IT HAS FOR TWENTY YEARS, THAT HE MAKES SEVEN DOLLARS AND HOUR.

IT WON'T NOTE THE THOUSAND DOLLAR BONUS GIVEN TO HIM SO HE WILL SHUT HIS MOUTH ABOUT WHAT HE HAD TO CLEAN UP THIS EVENING.

HE HAS NEVER BEEN THIS CLOSE TO A MURDER VICTIM.

HE HAS NEVER SEEN A WHAT WAS DONE TO THIS HUMAN.

FOR NOW THOUGH THE NIGHT WILL CONTINUE ON ITS STEAMY PATH, DIRTY ROADS WAITING FOR STREET

DOOR

THE DOOR CONTINUES ITS ASCENT.

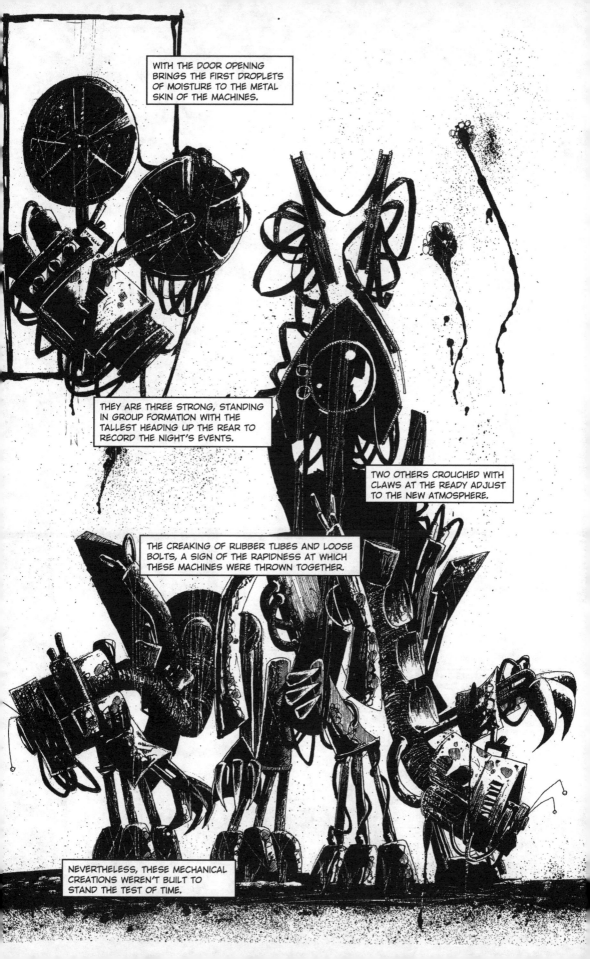

WITH THE DOOR OPENING BRINGS THE FIRST DROPLETS OF MOISTURE TO THE METAL SKIN OF THE MACHINES.

THEY ARE THREE STRONG, STANDING IN GROUP FORMATION WITH THE TALLEST HEADING UP THE REAR TO RECORD THE NIGHT'S EVENTS.

TWO OTHERS CROUCHED WITH CLAWS AT THE READY ADJUST TO THE NEW ATMOSPHERE.

THE CREAKING OF RUBBER TUBES AND LOOSE BOLTS, A SIGN OF THE RAPIDNESS AT WHICH THESE MACHINES WERE THROWN TOGETHER.

NEVERTHELESS, THESE MECHANICAL CREATIONS WEREN'T BUILT TO STAND THE TEST OF TIME.

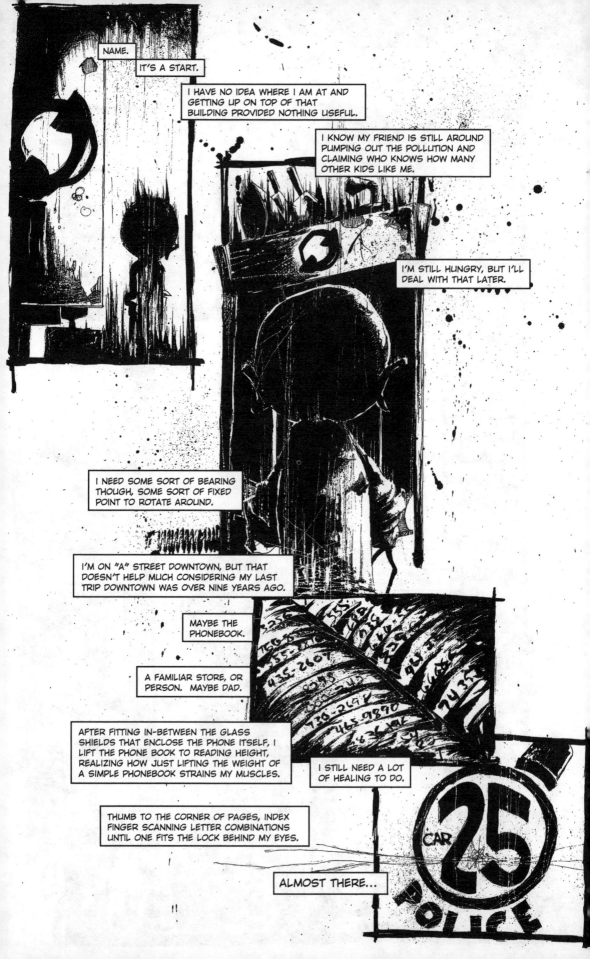

NAME.

IT'S A START.

I HAVE NO IDEA WHERE I AM AT AND GETTING UP ON TOP OF THAT BUILDING PROVIDED NOTHING USEFUL.

I KNOW MY FRIEND IS STILL AROUND PUMPING OUT THE POLLUTION AND CLAIMING WHO KNOWS HOW MANY OTHER KIDS LIKE ME.

I'M STILL HUNGRY, BUT I'LL DEAL WITH THAT LATER.

I NEED SOME SORT OF BEARING THOUGH, SOME SORT OF FIXED POINT TO ROTATE AROUND.

I'M ON "A" STREET DOWNTOWN, BUT THAT DOESN'T HELP MUCH CONSIDERING MY LAST TRIP DOWNTOWN WAS OVER NINE YEARS AGO.

MAYBE THE PHONEBOOK.

A FAMILIAR STORE, OR PERSON. MAYBE DAD.

AFTER FITTING IN-BETWEEN THE GLASS SHIELDS THAT ENCLOSE THE PHONE ITSELF, I LIFT THE PHONE BOOK TO READING HEIGHT, REALIZING HOW JUST LIFTING THE WEIGHT OF A SIMPLE PHONEBOOK STRAINS MY MUSCLES.

I STILL NEED A LOT OF HEALING TO DO.

THUMB TO THE CORNER OF PAGES, INDEX FINGER SCANNING LETTER COMBINATIONS UNTIL ONE FITS THE LOCK BEHIND MY EYES.

ALMOST THERE...

HIGH ABOVE THERE IS SOMETHING ELSE.

THROUGH A GLASS EYE ALL IS CAPTURED AND SENT OVER THE WAVES TO A RECEIVING DEVICE HIGH IN THE TOWER OF 'CIDE INC.

A TWITCHING ANTENNA TAKES IT ALL IN AND SPITS BACK A FLUID STREAM OF VIDEO TO THE GIRL IN THE CHAIR.

THE DRIPPING OF THE WATER IN THE NEXT ROOM AND THE SOUND OF THE MAN FIGHTING HIS WAY OUT OF THE SHOEBOX COUNT OFF TIME.

HER EYES AND THROAT WARM TO THE ALCOHOL AS SHE TYPES OUT THE COMMANDS TO BE SENT TO THE MACHINES SITTING ON TOP OF THE BUILDING HIGH ABOVE THE THREE FIGURES IN THE ALLEY.

THE FINAL TEST. LIVE SITUATION. LIVE AMMUNITION.

THE TOUCH OF A SWITCH AND THE MOTION IS SET.

A TWITCHING ANTENNA BACK ACROSS TOWN RECEIVES THE COMMAND AND THE MACHINES TAKE TO THE GROUND.

C'MON KID! MAKE THIS EASY ON YOURSELF!

NO AMOUNT OF WORDS OR THREATS IS GOING TO STOP SCHMALTZ NOW.

HE ESCAPED ONE HELL; WHO KNOWS WHAT OTHER MIGHT BE WAITING IF HE WERE TO SUCCUMB TO THE LAW.

YEAH, WE WOULDN'T WANT TO HAVE TO BEAT YOU TO A PULP!

DEEPER AND DEEPER INTO THE ALLEY; HE LEADS THEM ON A CHASE THAT SHOULD HAVE ENDED A FEW FEET INSIDE THE OPENING TO THE MAZE.

IT IS RAINING, THOUGH, AND THE USE OF DEADLY FORCE WOULD NOT BE JUSTIFIED.

THE GARBAGE STICKS TO SCHMALTZ'S BOOTS AND CLOTHES THE FURTHER HE GETS INTO THE ALLEY, AS IF BEING CONSUMED BY THE CITY ITSELF.

THEN, FOR AN INSTANT, THERE IS A NOISE VERY MUCH OUT OF PLACE.

THE SCRAPING OF METAL ON BRICK ARCHES THE SPINE AND SENDS THE COLD TO THE TIPS OF THE TEETH.

THE IMPACT OF THE MACHINES OF THE GROUND EQUATES TO THE ESTIMATED SOUND OF A THOUSAND TRASHCANS FALLING FROM THE GRAY CLOUDS.

THE SUDDEN JERK OF THE COPS HEAD TO SEE WHAT THE SOURCE WAS LEADS HIM DOWN A DAMNABLE PATH OF NO MORE BIRTHDAYS FOR THE KIDS AND NO MORE KISSES ON HIS WIFE'S CHEEK.

WITH THAT THE MACHINE CLOSEST TO HIM REMOVES HIS HEAD.

PEERING THROUGH THE DOOR WAS THE SOURCE OF THE METAL SCREAMS.

A SILHOUETTE VOID OF SYMMETRY, YET DISPLAYING HUNDREDS OF WIRES DRAPED LIKE A SPIDER WEB OVER ITS BODY STANDS IN THE DOORWAY.

THE KIDS ARE IN SHOCK, BUT BODY HEAT IS ON THE RISE AS THEY LOOK AT THE REASON ONE OF THEIR YOUNGEST NOW LAYS ON THE FLOOR WITH HIS BRAINS SLIDING ACROSS THE FLOORBOARDS.

THEIR INTERNAL THERMOMETERS BOIL OUT THE LAST OF THE MERCURY AND FLESH REACHES OUT FOR THE INSTRUMENT THAT WILL CARRY OUT THE RETALIATION.

PIPES. BOARDS. KNIVES. IF IT CAN BE HELD IT WILL DO.

THE MACHINE IS NOT PROGRAMMED WITH A SOPHISTICATED DEFENSE MODE SO THE BEST IT CAN DO IS TRY TO SHAKE IT OFF.

BOLTS FALL TO THE FLOOR. RUBBER CRACKS. WIRES LOOSEN WITH EVERY BLOW TO ITS BODY.

IT STILL MAINTAINS A CERTAIN INTEGRITY THOUGH, AN INTEGRITY THAT JUST MAY ALLOW IT TO LIVE LONG ENOUGH TO KILL OFF THE KIDS IF IT TRIES.

8A.M. NOTICES SOMETHING ENTIRELY DIFFERENT THOUGH.

HE SEES THE WEAKNESS.

WITH PIPE IN HAND, HE BECOMES THE KILLER IN THE HORROR FLICK WHO IS ABOUT TO CUT COMMUNICATION BETWEEN THE DAMSEL IN DISTRESS AND THE POLICE.

NO YOU WON'T BE FILING OUT THAT REPORT TONIGHT.

YOU ARE PUT ON HOLD BY THE POLICE DEPARTMENT AND JUST WHEN THEY ARE ABOUT TO COME BACK ON AND OFFER COMFORT AND

AND THAT BITCH IS MINE.

WITH NO CELLULAR MODEM TO OFFER A LINK TO NATALIE'S COMMANDS, THE MACHINE FALLS DEAD.

NOTHING MORE THAN LOOSE BOLTS, CRACKED RUBBER, AND FRAYED WIRE.

STANDING THERE IN TOTAL
AMAZEMENT BECAUSE HE
SEES ME ALSO.

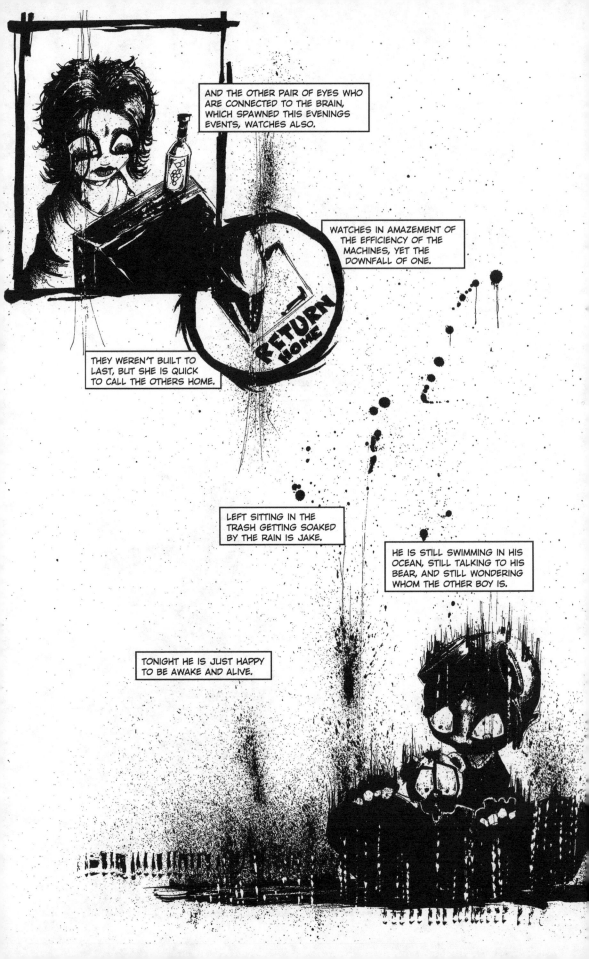

AND THE OTHER PAIR OF EYES WHO ARE CONNECTED TO THE BRAIN, WHICH SPAWNED THIS EVENINGS EVENTS, WATCHES ALSO.

WATCHES IN AMAZEMENT OF THE EFFICIENCY OF THE MACHINES, YET THE DOWNFALL OF ONE.

THEY WEREN'T BUILT TO LAST, BUT SHE IS QUICK TO CALL THE OTHERS HOME.

LEFT SITTING IN THE TRASH GETTING SOAKED BY THE RAIN IS JAKE.

HE IS STILL SWIMMING IN HIS OCEAN, STILL TALKING TO HIS BEAR, AND STILL WONDERING WHOM THE OTHER BOY IS.

TONIGHT HE IS JUST HAPPY TO BE AWAKE AND ALIVE.

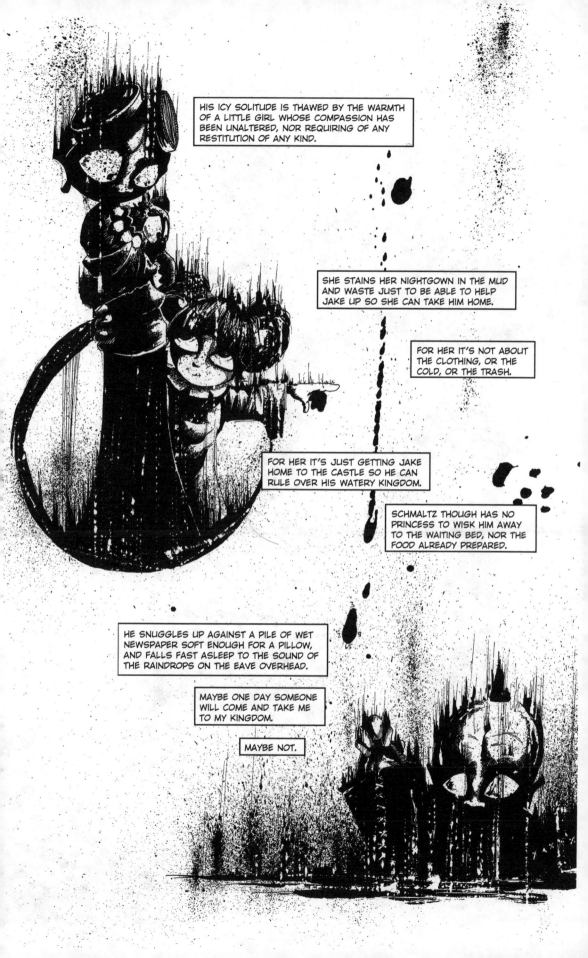

HIS ICY SOLITUDE IS THAWED BY THE WARMTH OF A LITTLE GIRL WHOSE COMPASSION HAS BEEN UNALTERED, NOR REQUIRING OF ANY RESTITUTION OF ANY KIND.

SHE STAINS HER NIGHTGOWN IN THE MUD AND WASTE JUST TO BE ABLE TO HELP JAKE UP SO SHE CAN TAKE HIM HOME.

FOR HER IT'S NOT ABOUT THE CLOTHING, OR THE COLD, OR THE TRASH.

FOR HER IT'S JUST GETTING JAKE HOME TO THE CASTLE SO HE CAN RULE OVER HIS WATERY KINGDOM.

SCHMALTZ THOUGH HAS NO PRINCESS TO WISK HIM AWAY TO THE WAITING BED, NOR THE FOOD ALREADY PREPARED.

HE SNUGGLES UP AGAINST A PILE OF WET NEWSPAPER SOFT ENOUGH FOR A PILLOW, AND FALLS FAST ASLEEP TO THE SOUND OF THE RAINDROPS ON THE EAVE OVERHEAD.

MAYBE ONE DAY SOMEONE WILL COME AND TAKE ME TO MY KINGDOM.

MAYBE NOT.

IT'S BEEN A LONG DAY FOR SOME OF US. A LONG DAY INDEED!

NOT FOR JAKE AND ERNIE.

NEVER WILL BE. IN FACT THE ONLY MUTUAL AIM WAS TO PURSUE THE NEXT SECOND IN THE INTEREST OF "FIXING" THE CLOCK.

STABILIZING.

A RECONCILED RELATIONSHIP.

SUSTAINING THE THREE OF THEM THROUGH A WORLD WITHOUT TIME.

WITHOUT A DOUBT ABOUT TOMORROW.

HASN'T HAPPENED YET THOUGH.

THAT DAY HASN'T GONE BY. AND THAT SOME FRETFUL MALAISE DIDN'T SET IN BY LOOKING TO TOMORROW.

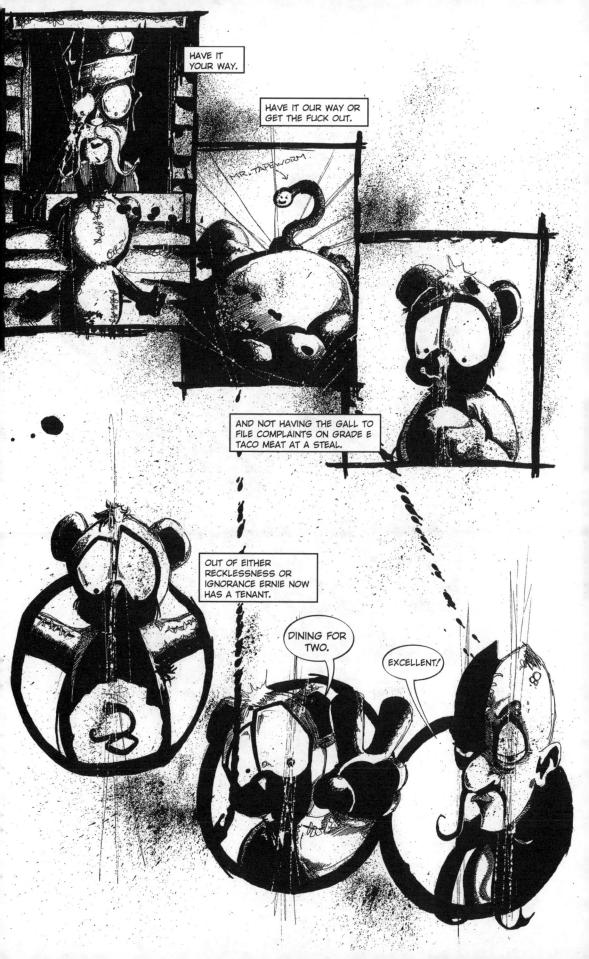

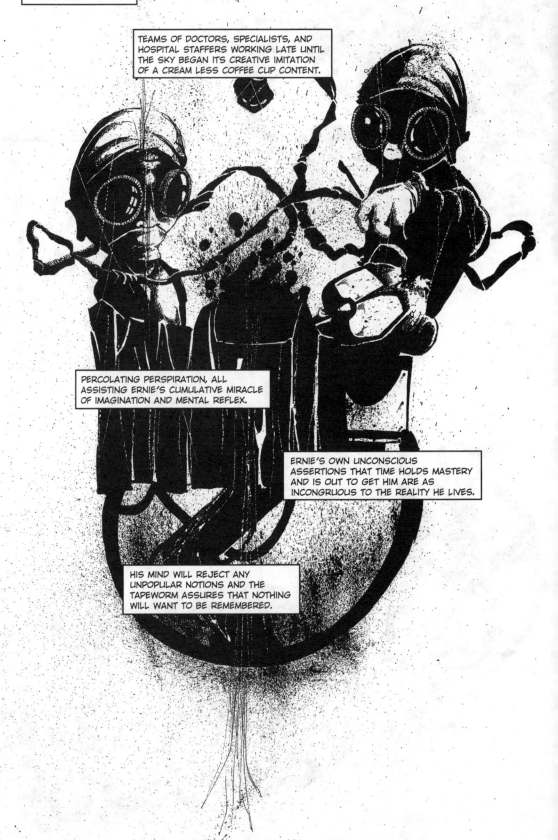

A LONG DREAM INDEED!

TEAMS OF DOCTORS, SPECIALISTS, AND HOSPITAL STAFFERS WORKING LATE UNTIL THE SKY BEGAN ITS CREATIVE IMITATION OF A CREAM LESS COFFEE CUP CONTENT.

PERCOLATING PERSPIRATION, ALL ASSISTING ERNIE'S CUMULATIVE MIRACLE OF IMAGINATION AND MENTAL REFLEX.

ERNIE'S OWN UNCONSCIOUS ASSERTIONS THAT TIME HOLDS MASTERY AND IS OUT TO GET HIM ARE AS INCONGRUOUS TO THE REALITY HE LIVES.

HIS MIND WILL REJECT ANY UNPOPULAR NOTIONS AND THE TAPEWORM ASSURES THAT NOTHING WILL WANT TO BE REMEMBERED.

MOMMY SO DELICATELY CRAFTS THAT FIRST
FOLD IN YOUR BRAIN, LIGHTLY, AND
WITHOUT THE USE OF HANDS NOR SHARP
SCALPELS SCRAPING FLAKES OF SKIN
ONTO THE FLOOR--AND CALLS IT BIRTH.

THAT FOLD ISN'T BUILT TO LAST. IT JUST
SERVES AS A SPRINGBOARD FOR ALL THE
OTHER TISSUE TO COIL AROUND AND TUCK
UNDER, LOSING TACT AS THE YEARS WEAR ON
AND FALLING VICTIM TO COLORS AND SHAPES
BROUGHT IN BY DEVELOPING EYES.

THE EVER CHANGING CIRCUMFERENCE
OF THE PUPIL CREATES THE MOOD
LIGHTING INSIDE YOUR SKULL, GIVING
SHADOWY DEFINITION TO THOSE FOLDS
WHICH WILL REMAIN IMMUTABLE.

TO THE MEMORIES WHICH WILL
COMFORT AND TORMENT FOR
YEARS TO COME.

FROM THAT FIRST INTERLOCKING OF MOMMY'S ARMS TO FORM THE SAFETY NET TO HOLD YOU CLOSE TO HER CHEST, TO THE WARMTH OF THE MILK IN THE BABY BOTTLE, AND EVEN TO THE AFGHAN GRANDMA MADE FOR YOU IN HER DUSTY HOME BEING PULLED UP TO YOUR NECK, STRONGER FOLDS IN YOUR BRAIN CONSUME WEAKER ONES, AND AT A FASTER RATE THAT THE WEAK SUBJUGATED THEIR ANCESTORS.

A SHROUD OF HISTORY FALLS UPON YOUR HEAD.

THEN THERE ARE THOSE WHOSE BRAIN SEEMS TO BE SMOOTH BEFORE YESTERDAY WAS DEFINED.

MOVING FORWARD, ELIMINATING THE FOLDS BY THE MINUTE.

THEY'VE KNOWN NOT A MOTHER, NOR A WARM AFGHAN, JUST THE VAT OF MOLTEN TRANSMITTERS WAITING FOR A MOLD TO BE POURED INTO, BUT NOT SITTING STILL AT THE SAME TIME.

THE INJECTIONS STILL SWIRL VIOLENTLY.

THE SEEMINGLY DREAM FILLED NIGHTS BEHIND TWITCHING EYES ARE LEFT UNNOTICED BY A BOY WHO AWAKENS THE NEXT MORNING ONLY TO ASK THE SAME QUESTIONS TO THE SAME TEDDY BEAR WHO

IT'S WHEN THE BOY FALLS ASLEEP TONIGHT THAT THIS BEAR DECIDES MAYBE IT'S TIME TO ANSWER HIS MASTER'S QUESTIONS.

HOPING THE SHIFT IN AIR TEMPERATURE AND MOVEMENT DOESN'T STIR THE BOY, THIS STUFFED MESSENGER SQUEEZES THROUGH THE CRACK IN THE WINDOW AND FALLS TO THE DUMPSTER BELOW.

THE ALLEY SWALLOWS THIS CRUSADER AND HIS MISSION WITH A MOUTH OF SHADOWS CAST BY THE DISCARDED.

THAT FAMILIAR STINK OF WORMS AND GARBAGE COVERS UP ANY PLEASANT THOUGHTS. THOUGHTS OF A MUCH NEEDED INJECTION.

THE DESTINATION LIES SLEEPING WITH NEWSPAPER OVER HIS HEAD, THE INTEGRITY OF THIS MAKE SHIFT HOME FAILING FAST.

HIS HEAD IS STICKY WITH PULP, FINGERS COATED IN MUD, THE RISING AND FALLING OF HIS CHEST PROVIDING THE PACE AT WHICH TO WORK AT.

RUNNING HIS HAND UP THE OPPOSING ARMS FUR AS IF TO PULL UP A SLEEVE, ERNIE SETS TO WORK.

THROUGH THOSE FOLDS OF FLESH AND AFGHAN, AND WITH THE SCRAPING OF BONE HE EXTRACTS WHAT HE CAME FOR.

THE NEEDLE GLOWS WITH FRESH DUPLICATES OF SCHMALTZ'S MEMORIES THAT ARE WAITING TO SOLIDIFY JAKE'S FOLDS.

ERNIE IS NOW TO PLAY MOTHER TO JAKE, CRAFTING THE SOFT TISSUE INTO YEARS OF TORMENT WITH A FEW SPLATTERS OF WARM PEACE.

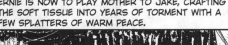

TURNING TOWARDS THE DIRECTION OF WHAT IS NOW HOME, ERNIE MOVES.

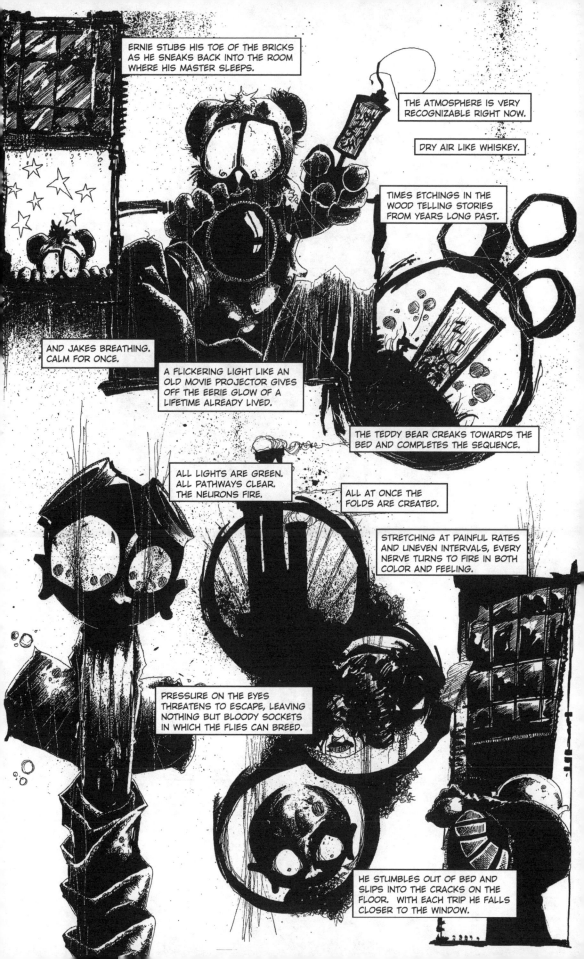

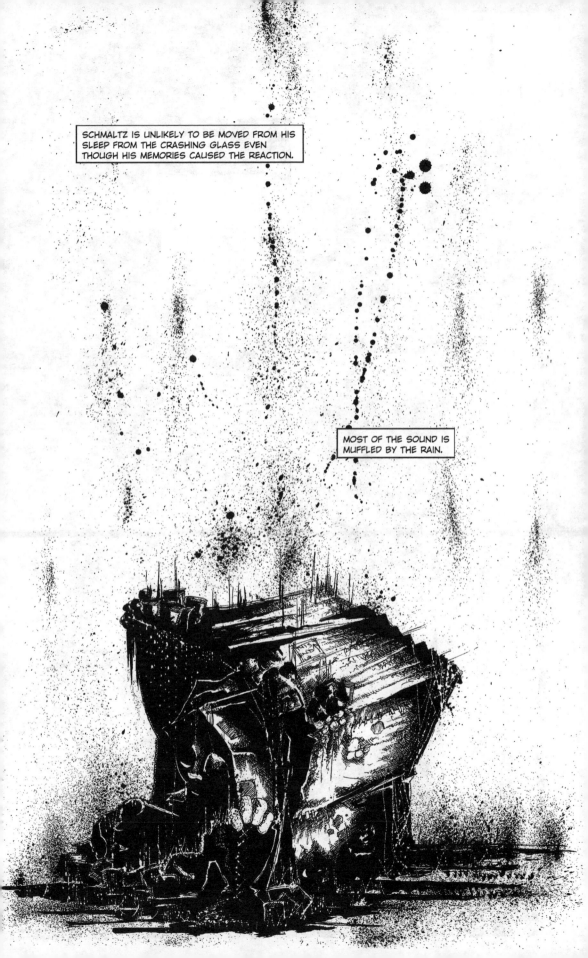

SCHMALTZ IS UNLIKELY TO BE MOVED FROM HIS SLEEP FROM THE CRASHING GLASS EVEN THOUGH HIS MEMORIES CAUSED THE REACTION.

MOST OF THE SOUND IS MUFFLED BY THE RAIN.

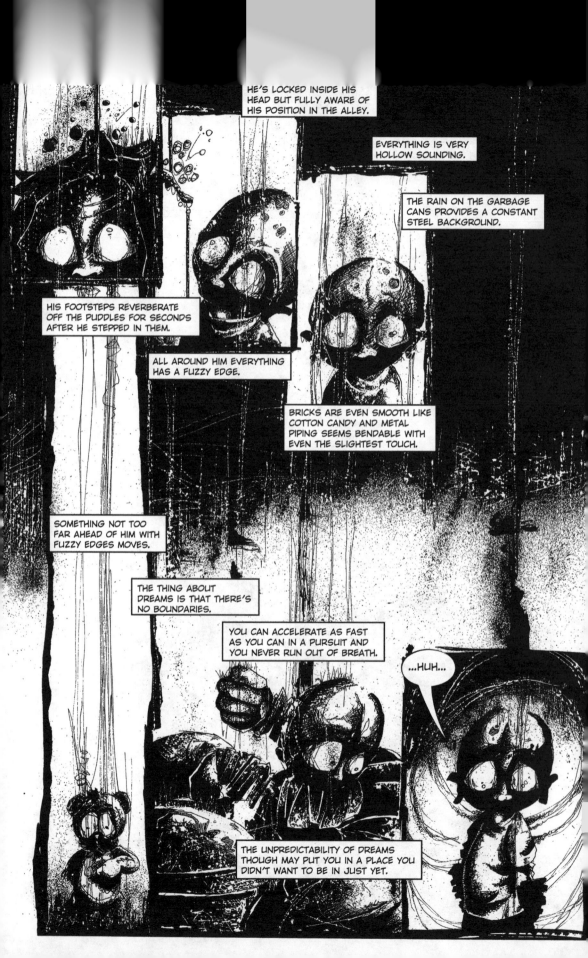

HE'S LOCKED INSIDE HIS HEAD BUT FULLY AWARE OF HIS POSITION IN THE ALLEY.

EVERYTHING IS VERY HOLLOW SOUNDING.

THE RAIN ON THE GARBAGE CANS PROVIDES A CONSTANT STEEL BACKGROUND.

HIS FOOTSTEPS REVERBERATE OFF THE PUDDLES FOR SECONDS AFTER HE STEPPED IN THEM.

ALL AROUND HIM EVERYTHING HAS A FUZZY EDGE.

BRICKS ARE EVEN SMOOTH LIKE COTTON CANDY AND METAL PIPING SEEMS BENDABLE WITH EVEN THE SLIGHTEST TOUCH.

SOMETHING NOT TOO FAR AHEAD OF HIM WITH FUZZY EDGES MOVES.

THE THING ABOUT DREAMS IS THAT THERE'S NO BOUNDARIES.

YOU CAN ACCELERATE AS FAST AS YOU CAN IN A PURSUIT AND YOU NEVER RUN OUT OF BREATH.

...HUH...

THE UNPREDICTABILITY OF DREAMS THOUGH MAY PUT YOU IN A PLACE YOU DIDN'T WANT TO BE IN JUST YET.

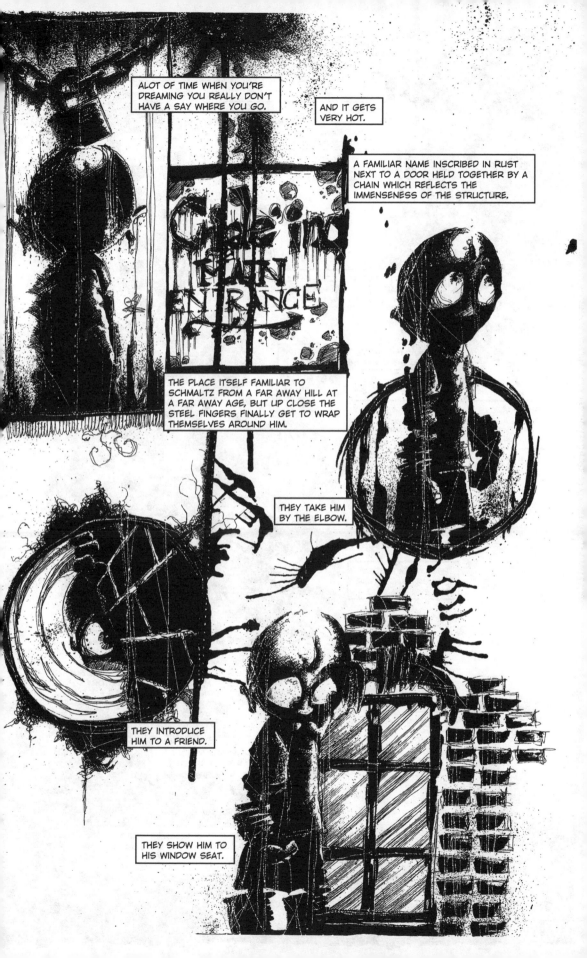

THE DIRT AND GREASE ON THE WINDOW IS THICK, BUT SCHMALTZ CAN STILL MANAGE A LOOK.

THE NOISES ARE VERY FAMILIAR AND MUCH, MUCH LOUDER.

MORE DETAILED AND CRISP THEN THOSE ECHOES FROM ACROSS THE HILL ON WHICH HE SAT MANY YEARS AGO, THEY START TO TAKE HOLD OF HIS HEAD.

THEY STILL TALK TO HIM THOUGH.

THEY STILL REMEMBER.

FIRST COME THE CONGRATULATIONS ON HIS ESCAPE FROM THE HOSPITAL AND THEN THEY TELL OF HOW MUCH THEY MISSED HIM.

THEY REMIND HIM OF WHAT HE DID TO HIS MOM.

THOSE VOICES CROWD AROUND HIM LIKE MEN IN A BAR AROUND A COUPLE OF WHISKEYS WITH STORIES FROM THE PAST TO ACCENTUATE THE FLOW OF THE LIQUID.

THE MEN WEAR GOGGLES AND OTHER PROTECTIVE GEAR.

SEEMS HARD TO HOLD THE SHOT GLASS WITH THOSE GLOVES.

THEY CARRY SLEDGE HAMMERS AND OTHER TOOLS OF MOLDING.

SCHMALTZ THEN REALIZES OTHERS WATCH HIM THROUGH THE GRIME.

AT FIRST STARTLED, HE BACKS UP QUICKLY, BUT NOT SO FAST AS TO MAKE SURE THESE FACTORY DENIZENS IMAGES ARE BURNED INTO HIS RETINAS FOREVER.

ANOTHER NOISE CLOSER TO HIM CAUSES HIS HEAD TO TWITCH.

SHIT!

A PIPE MUCH LARGER THAN A DRAIN FOR JUST RAINWATER STARTS TO SPUTTER.

ACCOMPANIED BY A GURGLING SOUND OF LIQUID LOOSENING UP THE CAKE OF DEBRIS ON THE INSIDE WALLS, THE TWITCHING BECOMES MORE VIOLENT.

AND THEN A HUMAN HEAD ROLLS OUT.

IT LOOKS AS IF THIS HEAD HAS BEEN TORN FROM THE BODY.

FLASHES OF PAST VIOLENCE ARE SET OFF IN SCHMALTZ'S HEAD IN THAT SAME SHADE OF MOVIE HOUSE BLUE HIS DREAMS ARE IN.

ONCE AGAIN SCHMALTZ REALIZES WHAT LIES BEHIND THIS BRICK ENCASING IS A FACTORY OF UNPARALLED VIOLENCE AND DISEASE.

THE FLIES COLLECT BY THE THOUSANDS ALONG WITH THE RATS TO DISPOSE OF ANY EDIBLE WASTE.

STEEL AND IRON, GLASS BREAKS. THE GLASS IS LOUDER THOUGH, AND SEEMINGLY ECHO LESS.

HE THEN REALIZES HE IS OUTSIDE OF HIS DREAM AND HE AWAKES.

SAME VAIN. SAME BOX.

HE GOES TOWARDS THE GLASS.

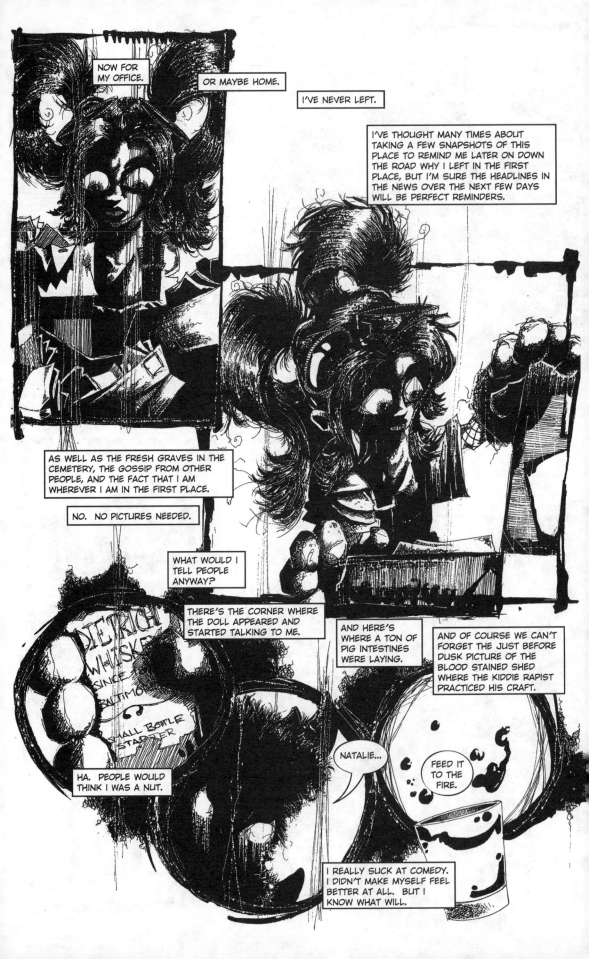

NOW FOR MY OFFICE.

OR MAYBE HOME.

I'VE NEVER LEFT.

I'VE THOUGHT MANY TIMES ABOUT TAKING A FEW SNAPSHOTS OF THIS PLACE TO REMIND ME LATER ON DOWN THE ROAD WHY I LEFT IN THE FIRST PLACE, BUT I'M SURE THE HEADLINES IN THE NEWS OVER THE NEXT FEW DAYS WILL BE PERFECT REMINDERS.

AS WELL AS THE FRESH GRAVES IN THE CEMETERY, THE GOSSIP FROM OTHER PEOPLE, AND THE FACT THAT I AM WHEREVER I AM IN THE FIRST PLACE.

NO. NO PICTURES NEEDED.

WHAT WOULD I TELL PEOPLE ANYWAY?

THERE'S THE CORNER WHERE THE DOLL APPEARED AND STARTED TALKING TO ME.

AND HERE'S WHERE A TON OF PIG INTESTINES WERE LAYING.

AND OF COURSE WE CAN'T FORGET THE JUST BEFORE DUSK PICTURE OF THE BLOOD STAINED SHED WHERE THE KIDDIE RAPIST PRACTICED HIS CRAFT.

DIETRICH WHISKEY
SINCE
BALTIMO
SMALL BOTTLE STARTER

HA. PEOPLE WOULD THINK I WAS A NUT.

NATALIE...

FEED IT TO THE FIRE.

I REALLY SUCK AT COMEDY. I DIDN'T MAKE MYSELF FEEL BETTER AT ALL. BUT I KNOW WHAT WILL.

IT'S STRANGE HOW WHEN YOU MAKE CHANGES IN YOUR LIFE YOUR WHOLE MIND FRAME CHANGES WITH IT ALMOST INSTANTLY. ALMOST AS IF IT WAS PREPARED.

I'M GUESSING IT'S COMING UP ON AUTUMN. SOME OF THE TREES LOOK LIKE THEY'D BE OLD MEN WITH CRUTCHES IF THEY WERE HUMAN AND I'VE SEEN SOME OF THE WORKERS COME IN WITH JACKETS. WHO KNOWS.

THAT'S WHAT I AM TALKING ABOUT. I'VE DECIDED TO ALTER MY LIFE AND NOW I AM WONDERING IF I SHOULD PACK A SWEATER SO AS NOT TO CATCH A CHILL.

IT'S ALWAYS BEEN SO HOT WERE I'VE BEEN AT. INSIDE MY HEAD AND OUT.

I WONDER IF THE SAME INVOLUNTARY ACTIONS INSIDE ME THAT PUSH ME TO WHERE I'VE BEEN AND HAVE HELPED PLAN THIS ARE GOING TO STAY WITH ME, OR IF I AM TO BE TOTALLY ALONE ONCE SEPARATED FROM THIS FACTORY.

A PART OF ME THINKS I WON'T GET FIFTY FEET FROM THE BACK LOADING DOCK BEFORE THE SMELL OF FRESH CUT GRASS AND BARBECUED CHICKEN DON'T MAKE ME TURN ILL.

I'M STRONG AS A BUSINESS WOMAN. I'VE PROVIDED A PLACE FOR LEGIONS OF FAMILIES TO SEND THEIR MEN EVERYDAY IN ORDER TO PUT FOOD IN FRONT OF THEM EVERY NIGHT.

I'VE GIVEN HOLIDAY BONUSES SO THAT THE TURKEY IS ENOUGH TO EVEN FEED THE DOG.

AND I'VE PROVIDED THE EXTRA MONEY FOR THAT BOTTLE OF WINE SO THAT ONCE IN A GREAT WHILE THE MEN OF THIS FACTORY CAN GO HOME AND ENJOY THAT UNCOMPROMISING LOVE FROM THEIR WIVES.

SURE, AS A BUSINESS WOMAN, I'VE BEEN A FINE PROVIDER OF MONEY. AS A BUSINESS WOMAN I HAVE MADE SURE THOSE WHO HAVE A NORMAL LIFE CAN LIVE IT. AS A HUMAN, THOUGH, I AM WEAK.

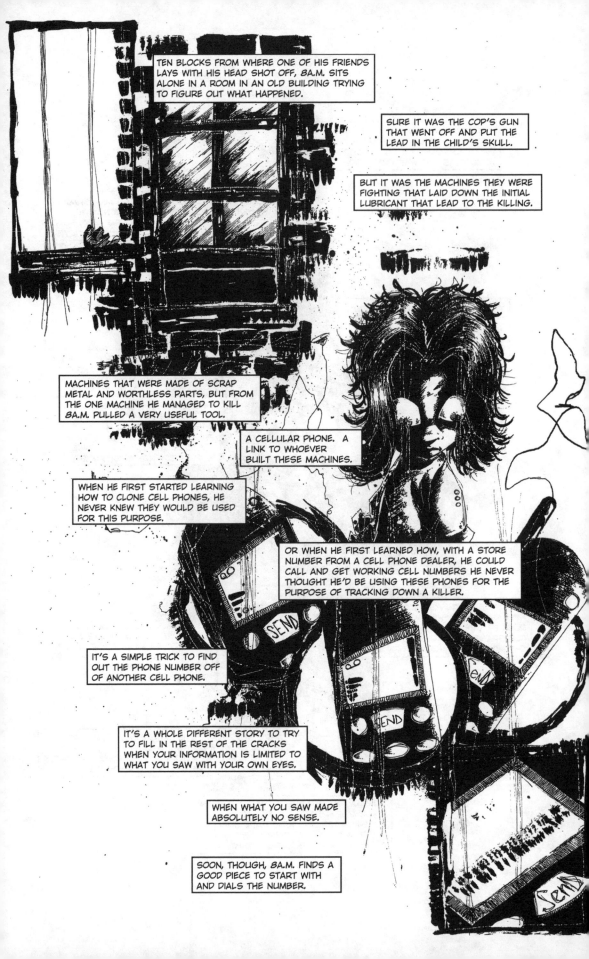

TEN BLOCKS FROM WHERE ONE OF HIS FRIENDS LAYS WITH HIS HEAD SHOT OFF, 8A.M. SITS ALONE IN A ROOM IN AN OLD BUILDING TRYING TO FIGURE OUT WHAT HAPPENED.

SURE IT WAS THE COP'S GUN THAT WENT OFF AND PUT THE LEAD IN THE CHILD'S SKULL.

BUT IT WAS THE MACHINES THEY WERE FIGHTING THAT LAID DOWN THE INITIAL LUBRICANT THAT LEAD TO THE KILLING.

MACHINES THAT WERE MADE OF SCRAP METAL AND WORTHLESS PARTS, BUT FROM THE ONE MACHINE HE MANAGED TO KILL 8A.M. PULLED A VERY USEFUL TOOL.

A CELLULAR PHONE. A LINK TO WHOEVER BUILT THESE MACHINES.

WHEN HE FIRST STARTED LEARNING HOW TO CLONE CELL PHONES, HE NEVER KNEW THEY WOULD BE USED FOR THIS PURPOSE.

OR WHEN HE FIRST LEARNED HOW, WITH A STORE NUMBER FROM A CELL PHONE DEALER, HE COULD CALL AND GET WORKING CELL NUMBERS HE NEVER THOUGHT HE'D BE USING THESE PHONES FOR THE PURPOSE OF TRACKING DOWN A KILLER.

IT'S A SIMPLE TRICK TO FIND OUT THE PHONE NUMBER OFF OF ANOTHER CELL PHONE.

IT'S A WHOLE DIFFERENT STORY TO TRY TO FILL IN THE REST OF THE CRACKS WHEN YOUR INFORMATION IS LIMITED TO WHAT YOU SAW WITH YOUR OWN EYES.

WHEN WHAT YOU SAW MADE ABSOLUTELY NO SENSE.

SOON, THOUGH, 8A.M. FINDS A GOOD PIECE TO START WITH AND DIALS THE NUMBER.

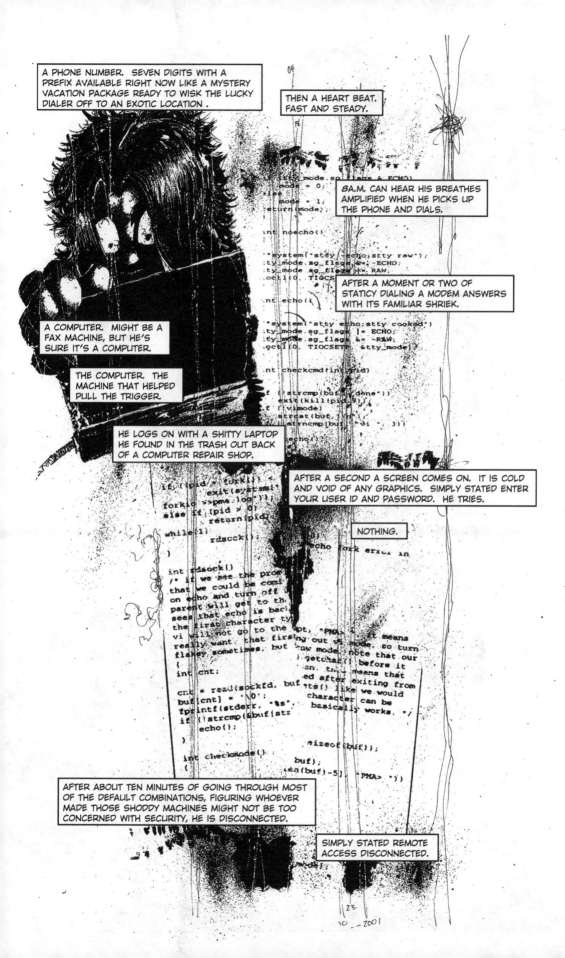

A PHONE NUMBER. SEVEN DIGITS WITH A PREFIX AVAILABLE RIGHT NOW LIKE A MYSTERY VACATION PACKAGE READY TO WISK THE LUCKY DIALER OFF TO AN EXOTIC LOCATION.

THEN A HEART BEAT. FAST AND STEADY.

8A.M. CAN HEAR HIS BREATHES AMPLIFIED WHEN HE PICKS UP THE PHONE AND DIALS.

AFTER A MOMENT OR TWO OF STATICY DIALING A MODEM ANSWERS WITH ITS FAMILIAR SHRIEK.

A COMPUTER. MIGHT BE A FAX MACHINE, BUT HE'S SURE IT'S A COMPUTER.

THE COMPUTER. THE MACHINE THAT HELPED PULL THE TRIGGER.

HE LOGS ON WITH A SHITTY LAPTOP HE FOUND IN THE TRASH OUT BACK OF A COMPUTER REPAIR SHOP.

AFTER A SECOND A SCREEN COMES ON. IT IS COLD AND VOID OF ANY GRAPHICS. SIMPLY STATED ENTER YOUR USER ID AND PASSWORD. HE TRIES.

NOTHING.

AFTER ABOUT TEN MINUTES OF GOING THROUGH MOST OF THE DEFAULT COMBINATIONS, FIGURING WHOEVER MADE THOSE SHODDY MACHINES MIGHT NOT BE TOO CONCERNED WITH SECURITY, HE IS DISCONNECTED.

SIMPLY STATED REMOTE ACCESS DISCONNECTED.

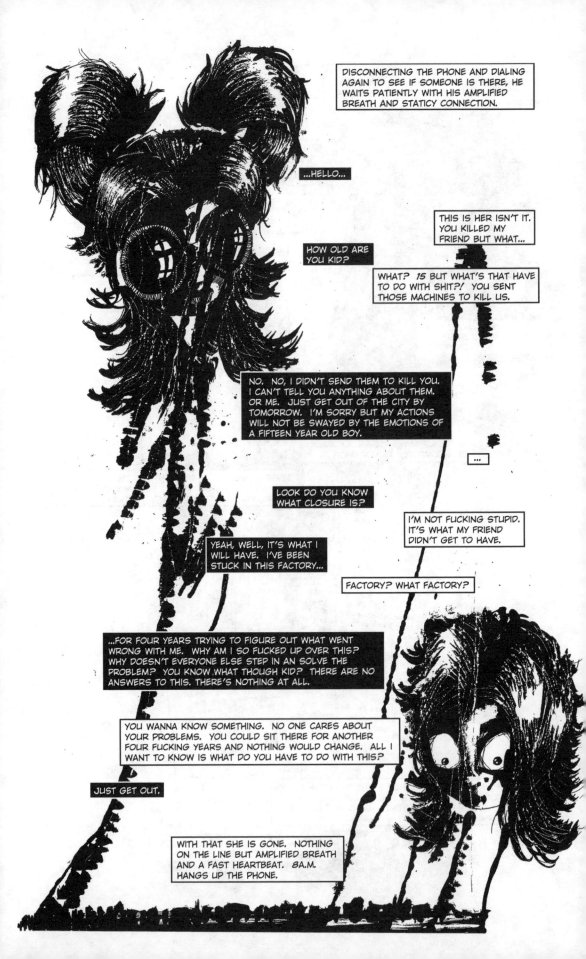

DISCONNECTING THE PHONE AND DIALING AGAIN TO SEE IF SOMEONE IS THERE, HE WAITS PATIENTLY WITH HIS AMPLIFIED BREATH AND STATICY CONNECTION.

...HELLO...

THIS IS HER ISN'T IT. YOU KILLED MY FRIEND BUT WHAT...

HOW OLD ARE YOU KID?

WHAT? 15 BUT WHAT'S THAT HAVE TO DO WITH SHIT?! YOU SENT THOSE MACHINES TO KILL US.

NO. NO, I DIDN'T SEND THEM TO KILL YOU. I CAN'T TELL YOU ANYTHING ABOUT THEM. OR ME. JUST GET OUT OF THE CITY BY TOMORROW. I'M SORRY BUT MY ACTIONS WILL NOT BE SWAYED BY THE EMOTIONS OF A FIFTEEN YEAR OLD BOY.

...

LOOK DO YOU KNOW WHAT CLOSURE IS?

I'M NOT FUCKING STUPID. IT'S WHAT MY FRIEND DIDN'T GET TO HAVE.

YEAH, WELL, IT'S WHAT I WILL HAVE. I'VE BEEN STUCK IN THIS FACTORY...

FACTORY? WHAT FACTORY?

...FOR FOUR YEARS TRYING TO FIGURE OUT WHAT WENT WRONG WITH ME. WHY AM I SO FUCKED UP OVER THIS? WHY DOESN'T EVERYONE ELSE STEP IN AN SOLVE THE PROBLEM? YOU KNOW WHAT THOUGH KID? THERE ARE NO ANSWERS TO THIS. THERE'S NOTHING AT ALL.

YOU WANNA KNOW SOMETHING. NO ONE CARES ABOUT YOUR PROBLEMS. YOU COULD SIT THERE FOR ANOTHER FOUR FUCKING YEARS AND NOTHING WOULD CHANGE. ALL I WANT TO KNOW IS WHAT DO YOU HAVE TO DO WITH THIS?

JUST GET OUT.

WITH THAT SHE IS GONE. NOTHING ON THE LINE BUT AMPLIFIED BREATH AND A FAST HEARTBEAT. 8A.M. HANGS UP THE PHONE.

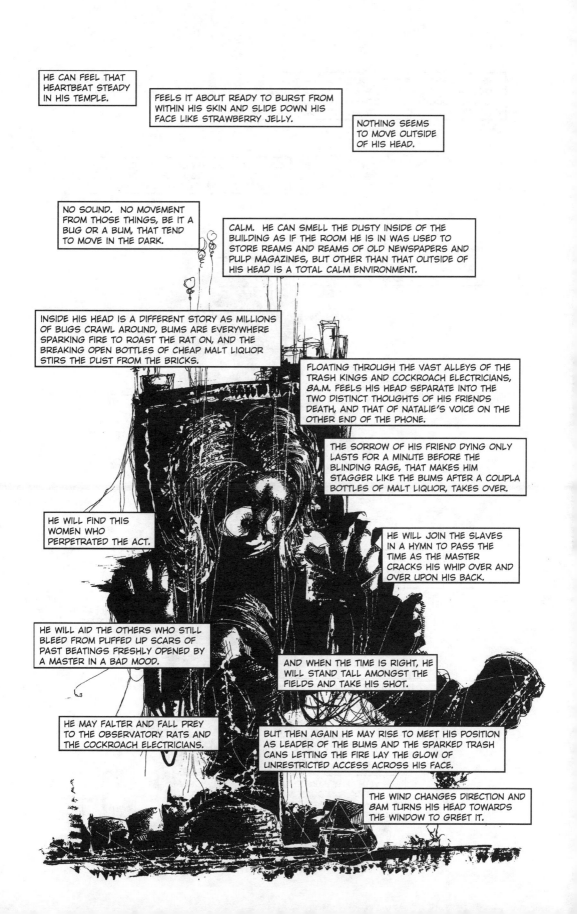

HE CAN FEEL THAT HEARTBEAT STEADY IN HIS TEMPLE.

FEELS IT ABOUT READY TO BURST FROM WITHIN HIS SKIN AND SLIDE DOWN HIS FACE LIKE STRAWBERRY JELLY.

NOTHING SEEMS TO MOVE OUTSIDE OF HIS HEAD.

NO SOUND. NO MOVEMENT FROM THOSE THINGS, BE IT A BUG OR A BUM, THAT TEND TO MOVE IN THE DARK.

CALM. HE CAN SMELL THE DUSTY INSIDE OF THE BUILDING AS IF THE ROOM HE IS IN WAS USED TO STORE REAMS AND REAMS OF OLD NEWSPAPERS AND PULP MAGAZINES, BUT OTHER THAN THAT OUTSIDE OF HIS HEAD IS A TOTAL CALM ENVIRONMENT.

INSIDE HIS HEAD IS A DIFFERENT STORY AS MILLIONS OF BUGS CRAWL AROUND, BUMS ARE EVERYWHERE SPARKING FIRE TO ROAST THE RAT ON, AND THE BREAKING OPEN BOTTLES OF CHEAP MALT LIQUOR STIRS THE DUST FROM THE BRICKS.

FLOATING THROUGH THE VAST ALLEYS OF THE TRASH KINGS AND COCKROACH ELECTRICIANS, 8A.M. FEELS HIS HEAD SEPARATE INTO THE TWO DISTINCT THOUGHTS OF HIS FRIENDS DEATH, AND THAT OF NATALIE'S VOICE ON THE OTHER END OF THE PHONE.

THE SORROW OF HIS FRIEND DYING ONLY LASTS FOR A MINUTE BEFORE THE BLINDING RAGE, THAT MAKES HIM STAGGER LIKE THE BUMS AFTER A COUPLA BOTTLES OF MALT LIQUOR, TAKES OVER.

HE WILL FIND THIS WOMEN WHO PERPETRATED THE ACT.

HE WILL JOIN THE SLAVES IN A HYMN TO PASS THE TIME AS THE MASTER CRACKS HIS WHIP OVER AND OVER UPON HIS BACK.

HE WILL AID THE OTHERS WHO STILL BLEED FROM PUFFED UP SCARS OF PAST BEATINGS FRESHLY OPENED BY A MASTER IN A BAD MOOD.

AND WHEN THE TIME IS RIGHT, HE WILL STAND TALL AMONGST THE FIELDS AND TAKE HIS SHOT.

HE MAY FALTER AND FALL PREY TO THE OBSERVATORY RATS AND THE COCKROACH ELECTRICIANS.

BUT THEN AGAIN HE MAY RISE TO MEET HIS POSITION AS LEADER OF THE BUMS AND THE SPARKED TRASH CANS LETTING THE FIRE LAY THE GLOW OF UNRESTRICTED ACCESS ACROSS HIS FACE.

THE WIND CHANGES DIRECTION AND 8AM TURNS HIS HEAD TOWARDS THE WINDOW TO GREET IT.

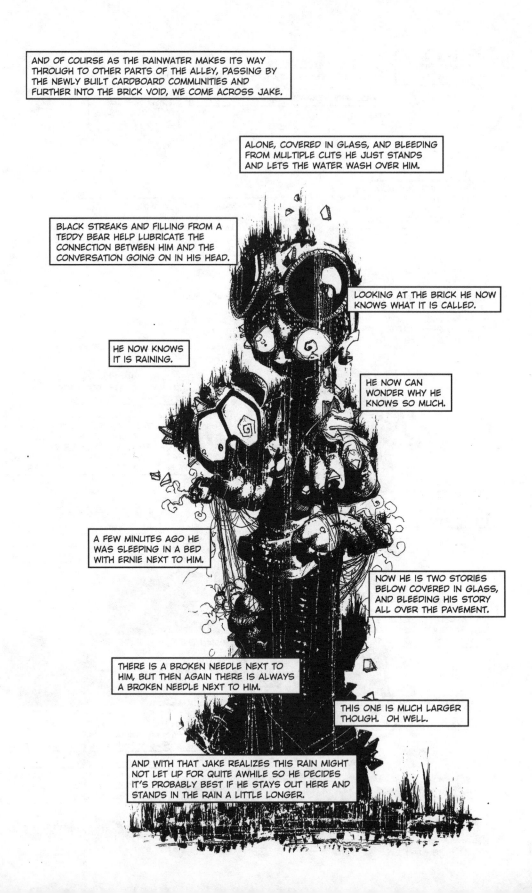

AND OF COURSE AS THE RAINWATER MAKES ITS WAY
THROUGH TO OTHER PARTS OF THE ALLEY, PASSING BY
THE NEWLY BUILT CARDBOARD COMMUNITIES AND
FURTHER INTO THE BRICK VOID, WE COME ACROSS JAKE.

ALONE, COVERED IN GLASS, AND BLEEDING
FROM MULTIPLE CUTS HE JUST STANDS
AND LETS THE WATER WASH OVER HIM.

BLACK STREAKS AND FILLING FROM A
TEDDY BEAR HELP LUBRICATE THE
CONNECTION BETWEEN HIM AND THE
CONVERSATION GOING ON IN HIS HEAD.

LOOKING AT THE BRICK HE NOW
KNOWS WHAT IT IS CALLED.

HE NOW KNOWS
IT IS RAINING.

HE NOW CAN
WONDER WHY HE
KNOWS SO MUCH.

A FEW MINUTES AGO HE
WAS SLEEPING IN A BED
WITH ERNIE NEXT TO HIM.

NOW HE IS TWO STORIES
BELOW COVERED IN GLASS,
AND BLEEDING HIS STORY
ALL OVER THE PAVEMENT.

THERE IS A BROKEN NEEDLE NEXT TO
HIM, BUT THEN AGAIN THERE IS ALWAYS
A BROKEN NEEDLE NEXT TO HIM.

THIS ONE IS MUCH LARGER
THOUGH. OH WELL.

AND WITH THAT JAKE REALIZES THIS RAIN MIGHT
NOT LET UP FOR QUITE AWHILE SO HE DECIDES
IT'S PROBABLY BEST IF HE STAYS OUT HERE AND
STANDS IN THE RAIN A LITTLE LONGER.

THE GLASS SMASHING
WAS NOT TOO FAR AWAY.

HE CAUGHT A GENERAL DIRECTION
OF ORIGINATION IN HIS EAR AND
STARTED IMMEDIATELY FOR IT.

NOTHING IS CLEAN DURING THE RAIN IN AN
ALLEY NO MATTER HOW MUCH WATER YOU
DUMP ON IT SO IT TOOK A BIT TO CLIMB
OVER THE SOGGY CARDBOARD AND TRASH.

PLUS THE SIX FOOT FENCE THAT
WAS IN HIS WAY DIDN'T HELP,
BUT SCHMALTZ MANAGED.

WITH THE SPEED AND GRACE OF A CAR
CRASH HE COVERED QUITE A BIT OF
ALLEY IN A FEW MINUTES WITHOUT
RECEIVING TOO MANY CUTS AND BUMPS.

PUSHING HIS WAY THROUGH THE CLOUD IN
FRONT OF HIS EYES STILL THERE FROM RECENT
SLEEP AND RECENT DREAM, HE ROUNDS THE
CORNER TO SEE THE SOURCE OF THE NOISE.

MORE TRASH CANS AND CLOUDED
VISION ARE IN HIS WAY BUT HE
CAN MAKE OUT THE FIGURE WHO
IS STILL COVERED IN GLASS.

A FAMILIAR FIGURE WITH
A FAMILIAR STUFFED
FRIEND TORN TO SHIT.

HE LOOKS DOWN AT HIS UNTIED BOOT
AND CRINGES AT THE THOUGHT OF
TOUCHING THE SLIME TO TIE IT.

SLOWLY THE MAN MAKES HIS WAY UP AND DOWN THE STREETS LIGHTING THE LAMPS.

IT'S HIS JOB AND HE DOES IT WITHOUT QUESTION AS TO IF HE COULD HAVE BEEN SOMETHING DIFFERENT. SOMETHING IMPORTANT.

WONDERS IF HE COULD BE THAT MUSICIAN HE ALWAYS WANTED TO BE, BLARING ON THE OL TRUMPET IN A BAND OF EIGHT.

THE CROWDS ROAR WHEN THE SONG FINISHES AND FRESH MEALS AND BOOZE FLOW ALL NIGHT AT THE AFTER PARTY.

SOME PEOPLE JUST WISH THEY COULD MAKE A DIFFERENCE IN THE WORLD BE IT GOOD OR BAD.

JUST TO SAY THEY HAD A PLAN AND EXECUTED IT.

THEN THERE ARE DOCTORS WHO SIT AND STARE AT A MONKEY SITTING IN FRONT OF A LAPTOP WAITING TO WRITE DOWN THE RESULTS WHEN THE MONKEY ACTUALLY SHOWS SOME SKILL IN OPERATING THE COMPUTER.

THOSE SAME SCIENTISTS CALL THE STREET BUM WHO READS POETRY ON A STREET CORNER FOR THE SHEER PLEASURE OF BRINGING THEIR VOICE TO THE MASSES CRAZY.

THE HOUSEWIFE, THE CARPENTER, THE COP, THE BAKER, THE YUPPIE, THE BUSINESSMAN LATE FOR A MEETING, THE COOK PONDERING THE DAYS SPECIALS, AND EVERYONE ELSE WHO DOES SOMETHING TO PASS THE TIME.

THE MAN WHO SLOWLY WALKS THE STREETS LIGHTING EACH LAMP.

TOMORROW WHEN THE SUN RISES AND THE LIGHT IS JUST OVER THE TOPS OF THE CARS IN THE STREETS THEY WILL ALL KNOW OF SOMEONE ELSE'S CONTRIBUTION TO THIS WORLD.

THEY WILL WISH THEY WERE HOME STARING AT OLD PHOTOGRAPHS AND DRINKING TEA AND WATCHING TV AND INDULGING IN EVERY OTHER DISTRACTING ACTIVITY WE AS HUMANS USE FOR ENTERTAINMENT.

WHEN THEY ARE CHOKING ON THEIR OWN TONGUES AND FEELING THEIR LUNGS FILL WITH BLOOD AFTER THE METAL IS INSERTED, THEY WILL WISH THEY WERE NO LONGER IN THIS CITY.

ON THIS PLANET. IN THIS UNIVERSE. AND DEFINITELY WISHING THEY NEVER KNEW THE GIRL NAMED NATALIE.

THREE HOURS AFTER THE FLOODGATES AT 'CIDE INC.
OPENED TO REVEAL NATALIE'S MASTER PLAN TO TEACH THE
CITY'S DENIZENS THAT OVER DEPENDENCY ON ELECTRONICS
AND MACHINERY COULD RESULT IN A SEVERING OF THE
UMBILICAL CORD THAT KEEPS THEM STABLE, NOTHING BUT
A GRAY DUST SETTLES OVER THE CITY.

THE INITIAL SHOCK OF THE KILLINGS, SNAPSHOTS
OF FLOWERS ON A SIDEWALK AND CHILDREN
HANGING FROM STOP SIGNS--ALMOST A
SEEMINGLY INTENDED PRO-CHOICE
ADVERTISEMENT--HAVE LEFT THERE SIGNATURES
BURNED INTO THE RETINAS OF THE SURVIVORS.

WHO KNOWS HOW MANY ARE STILL HIDING
IN THE CORNERS OF THE ABANDONED
SHOPS DROOLING AWAY THEIR LAST FEW
MOMENTS BEFORE THEY ARE FOUND BY THE
MACHINES AND DISPOSED OF.

SOME JUST SIT IN CANDLELIGHT AND
THUMB OLD PICTURES OF THEIR LOVED
ONES WHO HAVE ALREADY FALLEN.

OTHERS TRY THINGS THEY
NEVER GOT A CHANCE TO TRY
BECAUSE THEIR BUSY
SCHEDULES DIDN'T PERMIT IT...

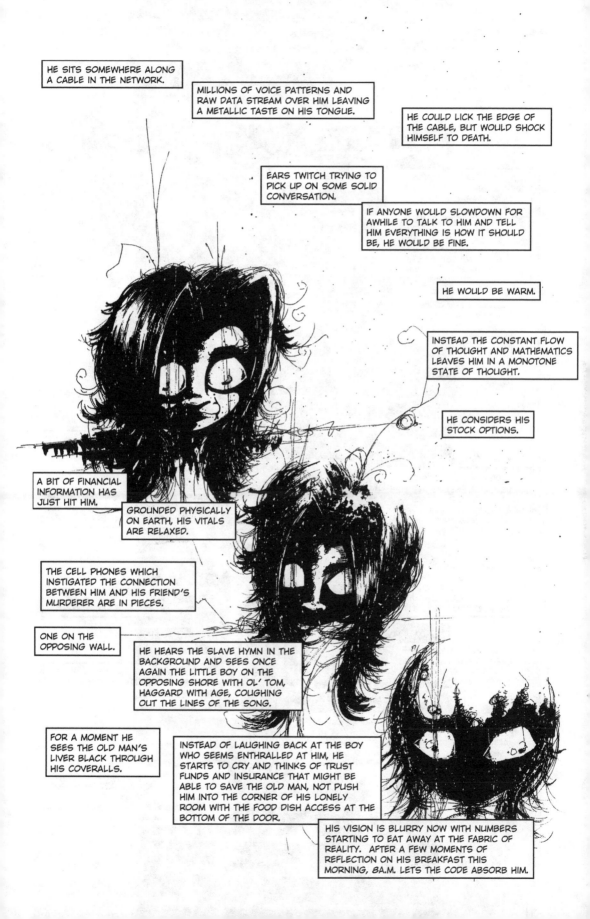

HE SITS SOMEWHERE ALONG A CABLE IN THE NETWORK.

MILLIONS OF VOICE PATTERNS AND RAW DATA STREAM OVER HIM LEAVING A METALLIC TASTE ON HIS TONGUE.

HE COULD LICK THE EDGE OF THE CABLE, BUT WOULD SHOCK HIMSELF TO DEATH.

EARS TWITCH TRYING TO PICK UP ON SOME SOLID CONVERSATION.

IF ANYONE WOULD SLOWDOWN FOR AWHILE TO TALK TO HIM AND TELL HIM EVERYTHING IS HOW IT SHOULD BE, HE WOULD BE FINE.

HE WOULD BE WARM.

INSTEAD THE CONSTANT FLOW OF THOUGHT AND MATHEMATICS LEAVES HIM IN A MONOTONE STATE OF THOUGHT.

HE CONSIDERS HIS STOCK OPTIONS.

A BIT OF FINANCIAL INFORMATION HAS JUST HIT HIM.

GROUNDED PHYSICALLY ON EARTH, HIS VITALS ARE RELAXED.

THE CELL PHONES WHICH INSTIGATED THE CONNECTION BETWEEN HIM AND HIS FRIEND'S MURDERER ARE IN PIECES.

ONE ON THE OPPOSING WALL.

HE HEARS THE SLAVE HYMN IN THE BACKGROUND AND SEES ONCE AGAIN THE LITTLE BOY ON THE OPPOSING SHORE WITH OL' TOM, HAGGARD WITH AGE, COUGHING OUT THE LINES OF THE SONG.

FOR A MOMENT HE SEES THE OLD MAN'S LIVER BLACK THROUGH HIS COVERALLS.

INSTEAD OF LAUGHING BACK AT THE BOY WHO SEEMS ENTHRALLED AT HIM, HE STARTS TO CRY AND THINKS OF TRUST FUNDS AND INSURANCE THAT MIGHT BE ABLE TO SAVE THE OLD MAN, NOT PUSH HIM INTO THE CORNER OF HIS LONELY ROOM WITH THE FOOD DISH ACCESS AT THE BOTTOM OF THE DOOR.

HIS VISION IS BLURRY NOW WITH NUMBERS STARTING TO EAT AWAY AT THE FABRIC OF REALITY. AFTER A FEW MOMENTS OF REFLECTION ON HIS BREAKFAST THIS MORNING, 8A.M. LETS THE CODE ABSORB HIM.

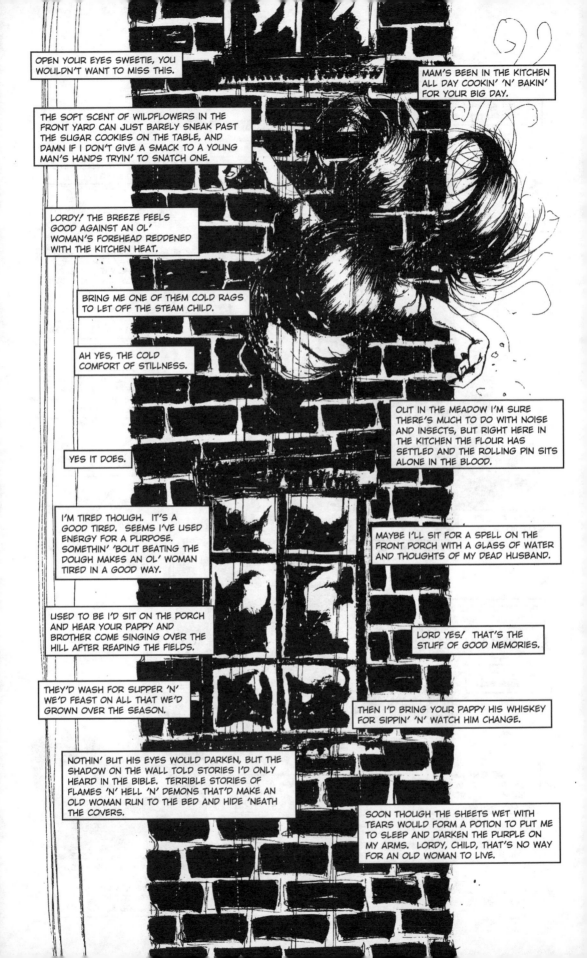

OPEN YOUR EYES SWEETIE, YOU WOULDN'T WANT TO MISS THIS.

MAM'S BEEN IN THE KITCHEN ALL DAY COOKIN' 'N' BAKIN' FOR YOUR BIG DAY.

THE SOFT SCENT OF WILDFLOWERS IN THE FRONT YARD CAN JUST BARELY SNEAK PAST THE SUGAR COOKIES ON THE TABLE, AND DAMN IF I DON'T GIVE A SMACK TO A YOUNG MAN'S HANDS TRYIN' TO SNATCH ONE.

LORDY! THE BREEZE FEELS GOOD AGAINST AN OL' WOMAN'S FOREHEAD REDDENED WITH THE KITCHEN HEAT.

BRING ME ONE OF THEM COLD RAGS TO LET OFF THE STEAM CHILD.

AH YES, THE COLD COMFORT OF STILLNESS.

OUT IN THE MEADOW I'M SURE THERE'S MUCH TO DO WITH NOISE AND INSECTS, BUT RIGHT HERE IN THE KITCHEN THE FLOUR HAS SETTLED AND THE ROLLING PIN SITS ALONE IN THE BLOOD.

YES IT DOES.

I'M TIRED THOUGH. IT'S A GOOD TIRED. SEEMS I'VE USED ENERGY FOR A PURPOSE. SOMETHIN' 'BOUT BEATING THE DOUGH MAKES AN OL' WOMAN TIRED IN A GOOD WAY.

MAYBE I'LL SIT FOR A SPELL ON THE FRONT PORCH WITH A GLASS OF WATER AND THOUGHTS OF MY DEAD HUSBAND.

USED TO BE I'D SIT ON THE PORCH AND HEAR YOUR PAPPY AND BROTHER COME SINGING OVER THE HILL AFTER REAPING THE FIELDS.

LORD YES! THAT'S THE STUFF OF GOOD MEMORIES.

THEY'D WASH FOR SUPPER 'N' WE'D FEAST ON ALL THAT WE'D GROWN OVER THE SEASON.

THEN I'D BRING YOUR PAPPY HIS WHISKEY FOR SIPPIN' 'N' WATCH HIM CHANGE.

NOTHIN' BUT HIS EYES WOULD DARKEN, BUT THE SHADOW ON THE WALL TOLD STORIES I'D ONLY HEARD IN THE BIBLE. TERRIBLE STORIES OF FLAMES 'N' HELL 'N' DEMONS THAT'D MAKE AN OLD WOMAN RUN TO THE BED AND HIDE 'NEATH THE COVERS.

SOON THOUGH THE SHEETS WET WITH TEARS WOULD FORM A POTION TO PUT ME TO SLEEP AND DARKEN THE PURPLE ON MY ARMS. LORDY, CHILD, THAT'S NO WAY FOR AN OLD WOMAN TO LIVE.

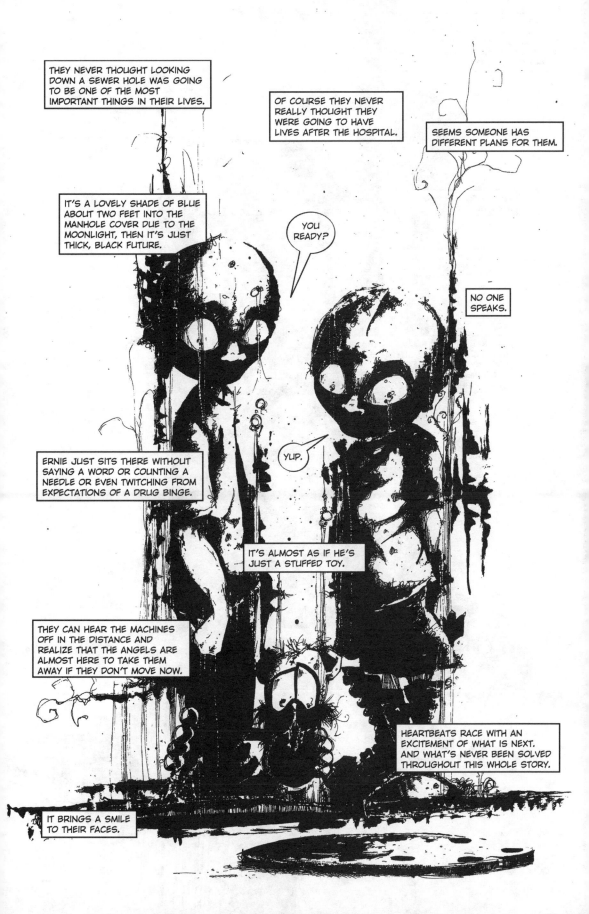

YEARS AGO WHEN HER FATHER DIED AT THE HANDS OF THIS FACTORY, SHE REALIZED THAT CONTROL DID NOT REST IN THE HANDS OF THOSE WHO OWNED THE FACTORY.

'CIDE INC. TOOK HER FATHER TO A PLACE WHERE THE HEARTS OF HUMANS ARE CONSUMED IN AN ATTEMPT AT ELIMINATING ORGANIC SUBSTANCE FROM A

HE SERVED HIS PURPOSE AND WAS FIRED.

NATALIE WOULD NOT FALL THE SAME WAY.

SHE KNEW IF SHE RELEASED THE MACHINES UPON THE CITY, THIS FACTORY WOULD BE TOO CONSUMED BY THE PLEASURE TO CARE IF SHE DISAPPEARED OR NOT.

YOU COULD ALMOST SEE THE PERMANENT SMILE ON THE FACE OF THE FACTORY.

IT ALMOST EXUDED THE SAME ENERGY OF A THIRTEEN YEAR OLD BOY AFTER HIS FIRST EJACULATION.

NATALIE WAS NEVER GOOD WITH THE BOYS THOUGH. TOO MUCH EFFORT.

WITH EVERYTHING IN ORDER IT WAS TIME TO CUT LOOSE THIS GUARDIAN OF BRICK AND MACHINERY.

NOW THE REAL FEAR SETS IN.

A FEW PRACTICES AT HUGGING, SMILING, AND HANDSHAKING, AND SHE IS READY TO FACE THE PUBLIC.

BEHIND HER IS SOON TO BE THE SCREAMS OF THE WORKERS, THE TIRELESS NIGHTS AND NIGHTMARES, AND A LIFE FULL OF PROBLEMS BUT NO RECOURSE.

ONE LAST LOOK OUT AT THE CITY IN FLAMES AND A NERVOUS TWITCH IN HER HAND LATER AND SHE IS OUT THE DOOR.

OUT TO FACE HUMANITY AND HOPEFULLY FORGE A LIFE AMONGST THOSE WHO SHE HAS JUST SLAUGHTERED A LARGE GROUP OF.

SEEMS IRONIC, BUT NEVERTHELESS NECESSARY TO CLEANSE HER MIND AND HOPEFULLY OPEN A FEW OTHERS UP.

AS SHE STEPS OUT THE DOOR AND FEELS DIRT FOR THE FIRST TIME IN AWHILE, SHE TAKES ONE LAST LOOK BACK AT THE FACTORY.

AT 'CIDE INC. THE SICKNESS SHE FEELS IS ENOUGH TO ALLOW HER TO NEVER FEEL THE CURIOSITY TO LOOK BACK.

OUT

A WHISPER OF THE FUTURE IS HEARD FROM WITHIN THE GRAY AREAS OF UNCERTAINTY.